Usborne Illustrated Originals

Heidi

Usboorne Illustrated Originals

Heidi

Johanna Spyri

Illustrated by
Elena Selivanova

Contents

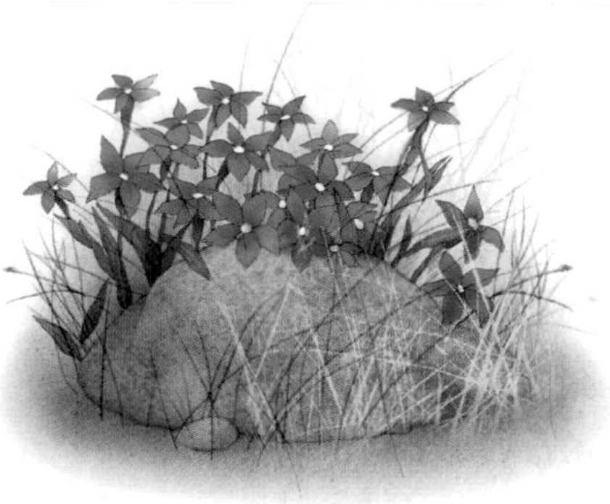

Chapter One

Up to the Alm Uncle

From the old town of Mayenfeld, a path leads to the foot of the mountains. At first, it winds through green and shady meadows, then as the land grows wilder, the path grows steeper, the air fragrant with the scent of mountain flowers. From here, the climb is steep to the towering summits above.

On a sunny morning in June, a stout young woman was climbing the mountain path, leading a child by the hand. The child's cheeks glowed through her brown skin, for on this hot day she was wrapped in enough clothes for a bitter winter. She couldn't have been much more than five years old, but it was difficult to see what she looked like. She was wearing two dresses, one over the other, and over these, wound round and round, a thick red shawl. She trudged uphill, a shapeless little figure, scuffing the ground with her heavy hobnailed boots.

After climbing for an hour or so, they reached a little hamlet known as Dörfli, halfway up the mountain. The woman was greeted by everyone, waving from windows and calling from doorways, for this was where she'd grown up. She didn't stop for a moment, however, but passed hurriedly on until she reached the last of the straggling houses at the end of the village. Here someone called from inside, "Wait a minute, Dete! If you are going further up the mountain, I'll come with you."

As Dete stood still, the little girl freed herself from her grasp, and sat down on the ground.

"Are you tired, Heidi?" asked Dete.

"No, I'm hot," replied Heidi.

"We're almost at the top. Keep going, Heidi, and take very big steps. It should only take another hour," Dete said encouragingly.

At that moment, a plump, pleasant-faced woman came out of a house to join them. Immediately she and Dete began walking on, while Heidi stood up and followed on behind. Dete and her friend were soon chatting away about everybody and everything in Dörfli.

"Where are you taking the girl, Dete?" asked her friend, after a little while. "Is she your sister's orphan?"

"Yes," replied Dete. "I'm taking her up to the Alm Uncle. She's going to live with him, now."

She trudged uphill, a shapeless little figure, scuffing the ground with her heavy hobnailed boots.

"What, leave this child with the Alm Uncle? You must be out of your mind, Dete! How can you think of such a thing? But you won't get the chance. He'll send you both packing."

"He can't do that. He's the child's grandfather, and must take care of her. I've always looked after her, but it's his turn now. I've been offered a wonderful job, Barbel, and I don't mean to turn it down because of her. He must do his duty."

"Yes, if he were like other people," replied Barbel anxiously. "But you know the kind of man he is. He won't know what to do with the child. She'll run away from him."

Dete didn't answer, so Barbel went on with her questions. "Where is your new job?" she asked.

"I'm going to Frankfurt," explained Dete, proudly. "I've been promised a job with a very good family there. I met them in Ragaz, at the hotel where I worked as a chambermaid. I took such good care of their rooms and their comfort last year, they wanted to take me back with them. But I couldn't go because of Heidi. Now they have come again, and repeated their offer – and this time I mean to accept it."

"Well, I wouldn't like to be in this child's shoes, not for anything," exclaimed Barbel. "No one knows what the Alm Uncle's doing up there, as he never has anything to do with any of us. He never goes to church, and when he does come to Dörfli, every once in a while, we're all terrified of him. Just the sight of him is alarming enough, with that great big stick he always carries, and his bushy eyebrows and his horrid long beard!"

"But still," said Dete defiantly, "he is Heidi's grandfather, and he must take care of her. If she comes to any harm, he will have to answer for it, not me."

"I should so like to know," said Barbel inquiringly, "what that old man has on his conscience. It must be something very wicked that makes him so angry, and keeps him up there on the mountain, with never a soul to speak to. They say all sorts of strange things about him. But it's hard to tell what's true, and what's just gossip. You must know the truth from your sister, don't you?"

"Yes I do, but I'm not telling. Alm Uncle would be furious if he ever found out I'd said anything!"

But Barbel was too full of curiosity about the Alm Uncle to leave it there. For a long time, she had wondered why he looked so fierce, and why he lived all alone on the mountain. No one would say a word against him, she noticed, almost as if they were afraid. And why did all the people of Dörfli called him Alm Uncle? He couldn't be uncle to them all, but no one called him anything else and even she did the same.

Barbel had only lived in Dörfli since her marriage, so she wasn't yet familiar with all that had happened in the village. But her friend Dete had been born in Dörfli, and had lived there until her mother's death a year ago. Barbel was determined not to lose this opportunity to find out more.

Slipping her arm through Dete's, she said coaxingly, "Only you can tell me the real truth about the Alm Uncle. Do tell me. What's the matter with the old man? Have people always been afraid of him? Has he always seemed to hate everyone?"

"Well, I'm twenty-six and he's seventy," Dete pointed out, "so I can't know for sure if he's always been like this. But you're right, I know all kinds of things about him, as he and my mother both came from the same place. But I don't want to tell you unless I can be sure it won't go round the whole valley."

"Oh Dete!" replied Barbel, half offended. "What do you mean? I can keep a secret, if I have to. Do tell me! I promise you won't regret it. I won't tell a soul."

"Well, I will, but make sure you keep your word," warned Dete.

She looked back, to see if Heidi was near enough to hear what they said, but the child was nowhere to be seen. She must have fallen behind some time ago, but they were too busy talking to notice. Dete stopped, and looked about in every direction. The path twisted and turned, this way and that, but she could follow it all the way to Dörfli. There was no one in sight.

"I see her!" exclaimed Barbel. "Down there!" And she pointed to a spot quite far from the mountain path. "She's climbing up the cliff with Peter and his goats. I wonder why he's so late today? But isn't that lucky for us! Now you can go on with your story while he looks after the child."

"Heidi may be only just five, but she can take care of herself," said Dete. "She notices everything that goes on and can make the best of things. And that will stand her in good stead, after all, for the Alm Uncle only has his two goats now, and the Alm hut."

"Did he once have more?" asked Barbel.

"Oh yes," replied Dete. "He had one of the very best farms in the area. He was the elder son, and had only one brother, who was quiet and decent. But the Alm Uncle lived a fast life. He was always playing the gentleman, always in bad company. No one knew anything about his friends, or where they were from. He gambled away his property, and when everyone found out, his father and mother died of grief, one after the other. His younger brother was left as poor as a beggar, and went off in anger. No one every heard from him again."

"What did the Alm Uncle do then?" asked Barbel, hanging on every word.

"Well," said Dete, carring on with her tale, "when he realized he had ruined his reputation, and that he had nothing left, the Alm Uncle disappeared too. At first, no one knew where he had gone, but after a while it was said he'd joined the army, and gone to Naples.

"Nothing more was known for twelve years or so. Then one day he appeared again, with a half-grown boy. They said he'd met his wife in the South, but that she'd died soon after having the boy. The Alm Uncle tried to find a home for his son among his relatives. But do you know what everyone did?"

Barbel shook her head.

"They closed their doors against him," said Dete, dramatically. "No one would have anything to do with him. That was when he came to Dörfli, and lived there with his boy. He must have had some money, I suppose, for he had his son, Tobias, trained up as a carpenter."

"What was Tobias like?" asked Barbel.

"Wait a minute! I can only tell one thing at a time," said Dete, stopping to rest for a moment on the steep mountain path. "Give me a moment while I catch my breath. Now, where was I?"

"Tobias..." prompted Barbel.

"Oh yes! He was a decent fellow, and everyone in Dörfli liked him. But no one trusted the Alm Uncle. It was said that he'd run away from the army in Naples because he'd killed a man! Not in a battle, you realize, but in a brawl. But even though everyone turned away from him, we accepted him as part of our family. My great-grandmother and his grandmother were sisters, so we called him Uncle. And as we're related to practically everyone in Dörfli, the whole village soon called him Uncle, too. Since he went to live up on the Alm pastures, he became known as the Alm Uncle."

"But what happened to Tobias?" said Barbel, wanting to know every detail.

"He was sent away to learn his trade, and when he had finished he returned to Dörfli and married my sister, Adelheid. They had always liked each other and lived very happily together. But two years after their marriage he was killed in a terrible accident. He'd been helping to build a house and a beam had fallen on him and crushed him. When they brought his body home, Adelheid fell ill from the shock and sorrow of it all. She went down with a fever and never recovered.

"Adelheid had always been rather delicate. When we were children she would fall into swoons and we couldn't tell if she was awake or asleep. Only two weeks after Tobias' death, we buried Adelheid. That was when the gossip started... Everyone said to themselves, and then out loud, that the fate of these two was the Uncle's punishment for his wicked life. Our pastor talked to him too, and urged him to repent. But it was no good. He only grew more fierce and sullen and spoke to no one. In the end, everyone avoided him.

"Soon after, we heard that he had gone up to live on the Alm, never coming down unless he had to. Since then he has lived alone on the mountainside, at war with God and man.

"My mother and I took in Adelheid's little girl. Heidi was only a year old at the time. Then, last summer, when my mother died, I decided to go to Ragaz to earn some money. I couldn't take Heidi with me, of course, so I paid old Ursel, who lives in the village above Dörfli, to look after her. I stayed on at Ragaz through the winter, for I can sew and mend, so I had no difficulty finding work. Early in the spring, the Frankfurt family stayed at the hotel again and asked me to go back with them. We leave the day after tomorrow. It's a very good job, I can tell you."

"And you're going to leave the child up there with that old man?" said Barbel reproachfully. "I can't understand what you're thinking of, Dete."

"What do you mean by that?" snapped Dete. "I have done my fair share for the child. What more can I do? I can't take a five-year old to Frankfurt with me. But where are you going, Barbel?" she asked, as her friend had begun walking away from her, leaving the mountain path. "We're halfway up the Alm."

"We've reached the place I wanted," said Barbel. "Goat Peter's mother does spinning for me in winter, and I wanted to talk to her about it. So goodbye, Dete! Good luck to you!"

Dete waved to Barbel, then stood watching as her friend went towards a small, wooden hut, which stood a little way from the path. Dete hadn't spotted it before, as it was nestled in a little hollow. It looked tumbledown and weather-worn, and when the south wind blew, it made the walls tremble and the windows rattle. It was lucky the hut stood halfway between Dörfli and the Alm, in its little hollow. Had it been built higher up, the hut could easily have been blown by one gust of the mountain winds into the valley below.

This was Peter the goatherd's home. He was

eleven, and his job was to drive the goats from Dörfli up to the Alm every morning. There they grazed on the short, succulent grasses and mountain plants. In the evening he led the goats down into Dörfli again, whistling through his fingers for the goats' owners to come to collect them. Most of the owners sent their children, small boys and girls, who would throng to the little square, unafraid of the gentle goats. For this short time, Peter was able to play with friends his own age. For the rest of the day he was alone with the goats on the mountain pastures.

He spent very little time at home with his mother and his blind old grandmother, who lived with them. He would rise early, bolt down his breakfast of bread and milk, and return late, spending as long as possible playing with the other children in the square in Dörfli. He got home just in time to gobble down his supper of bread and milk again, before tumbling, exhausted, into his bed.

Peter's father had been a goatherd before him, and, like him, had been known to everyone as Goat Peter, but he had been killed while felling trees some years before. His mother's real name was Brigitte, but she was always called Goat Peter's mother. And for everybody far and wide, old and young, the blind old grandmother was simply 'Grandmother'.

Dete stood waiting anxiously for Heidi and Peter to appear, looking in every direction, but the children and the goats were nowhere to be seen. After a little while, she climbed still higher to get a better view of the valley. She looked around, growing more and more impatient.

But the children had strayed far from the path. Peter always went his own way up the mountain, searching out the best spots where his goats could find bushes and leaves to nibble. His route twisted this way and that, over rocks and boulders and tufts of grass. At first, Heidi climbed after him, puffing and panting, but refusing to give up. She felt hot and heavy in all her layers of clothes, and it took all her strength just to keep up with him.

She never complained, however, but watched Peter carefully as he sprang up the slopes on his bare feet, his light, loose trousers allowing him to make easy, carefree strides. Then she watched the goats, climbing and leaping even more nimbly over bush and boulder, and even up the steepest cliffs, on their thin, slender legs.

Suddenly, Heidi sat down and pulled off her shoes and stockings in a hurry. Then she stood up again, threw off her thick red shawl, unbuttoned her dress and took it off. She still had another underneath, for Dete had made her wear her best dress on top of her everyday one, to save herself having to carry it. In a twinkling, Heidi tore off her everyday dress too, and stood in her light petticoat, waving her bare arms in delight.

Then she folded all her clothes together into a neat little heap and, leaving them, ran up after the goats to Peter.

Peter hadn't been paying attention, but when Heidi sprang up beside him in her petticoat, he grinned at her. Then, looking

back, he saw the little heap of clothes, and his grin became wider, until his mouth seemed to stretch from ear to ear. But he said never a word.

Now that Heidi felt free and comfortable, she began chatting away to Peter, asking him question after question. She wanted to know how many goats he had, where he was taking them, and what he would do when he got there. At last, however, the children and the goats reached the hut. When Dete caught sight of the little company of climbers, she shouted out, "What are you doing, Heidi? Just look at you! What have you done with your two dresses and the shawl? And the new shoes I bought you to wear on the mountain, and the new stockings I knit for you myself? Are they all gone?"

Heidi pointed calmly down the mountainside to the little pile of clothes. "There they are," was all she said.

Dete looked, and following the direction of the chubby finger, she saw a little heap of something, with a red speck on top. She supposed that must be the shawl.

"You mischievous child!" she cried crossly. "What are you thinking of? Why have you taken all your things off?"

"I don't need them," Heidi replied, not sounding the least bit sorry for what she had done.

"Oh, you thoughtless child! Foolish Heidi! Don't you know anything?" said Dete, scolding and complaining at the same time. "Who will go down and get them? It will take at least half an hour to get there and back again. Come, Peter, run down and fetch them for me! Don't just stand there as if you were nailed to the spot."

"I'm late as it is," said Peter slowly, without moving. He thrust his hands deeper into his pockets.

"Well, you won't get very far if you keep standing there gawping," Dete shouted. "Come now," she went on, trying to sound more persuasive, "if you fetch the clothes, I'll give you something nice. Do you see this?"

She held up a coin to him, which sparkled in the sun. With a bound he was off down the mountain, taking the shortest route, reaching the clothes in giant leaps and strides. He seized them in his arms, and was back again so quickly, Dete could only stare in amazement.

"There!" she said, handing him the coin. "You have earned it," she added, thinking he deserved the praise.

Peter quickly stuck the coin deep into his pocket, his face beaming with pleasure. He wasn't used to such riches.

"Heidi, put your everyday dress back on. Peter, you can carry the rest of the bundle up to the Alm Uncle's. You're going that way with your goats, anyway," said Dete. Without waiting for an answer, she began to climb the steep path that led up from behind the goatherd's hut. Peter followed her willingly, carrying the bundle under his left arm, and swinging the long stick he used for the goats in his right. Heidi and the goats leaped along beside him.

After three quarters of an hour, the party reached the top of the Alm, where the old Uncle's hut stood, exposed to every wind that blew, but also getting every ray of sunshine, and a beautiful view of the valley below. Behind the hut stood three tall, very old pine trees, with long, thick, untrimmed branches. Beyond, the mountain continued to climb, first through beautiful green slopes, then over thickly strewn boulders, and at last, rising up, up over them all, were the bald, steep pinnacles.

On the side of his hut overlooking the valley, the Alm Uncle had placed a bench, fastened securely to the side of the hut. He was sitting there now, his pipe in his mouth, his hands resting on his knees. Calmly, he watched the approach of the children, the goats, and last of all Dete, who had long been overtaken by the others.

Heidi reached the top first. She walked straight towards the old man. "Good morning, Grandfather," she said, and stretched out her hand to him.

"Well, well, what's that supposed to mean?" he asked gruffly. He shook Heidi's hand, however, looking at her searchingly.

Heidi returned his look with equal steadiness, not once letting

her eyes swerve from his face. Grandfather was such a curious-looking man. He had a big white beard and thick bushy eyebrows. She wanted to stare and stare.

Dete and Peter now stood beside Heidi, Peter looking on to see what would happen next.

"Good day, Uncle," said Dete, stepping up. "I've brought Tobias and Adelheid's child. You will hardly recognize her, for you haven't seen her since she was a year old."

"What has that child got to do with me?" asked the old man. "You there!" he called out to Peter. "Be off with your goats. You're late this morning. And don't forget to take mine with you."

Peter obeyed him instantly. The look the Alm Uncle gave him was enough to make him disappear at once.

"Heidi has to stay here with you," insisted Dete. "I've looked after her for four years. Now it's your turn."

"Ha!" said the old man, casting a withering glance at Dete. "And what am I supposed to do when she begins to cry and whimper for you? I know what these foolish little creatures are like. What do you suggest I do then?"

"That's your business," said Dete. "No one told me what to do with her, when she was left on my hands as a baby. And I had enough to do as it was, looking after my mother and myself. Now I have to go to Frankfurt to earn some money, and I can't take her with me. You are her nearest relation. If you won't keep her, do as you think best for her. But if anything happens to her, it will be on your conscience, and I should think you have enough to answer for already."

Dete's own conscience was far from easy. She'd worked herself into a passion, and said more than she'd really meant to. As she uttered these last words, the Alm Uncle stood up, and looked at her so fiercely that she drew back. He stretched out his arm. "Go back to where you came from," he ordered, "and don't show your face here again in a hurry."

"Then goodbye, and to you too, Heidi," cried Dete. She turned and ran down the mountainside. She didn't stop once, all the way to Dörfli. She was so agitated she felt as if she had a steam-engine at work inside her, driving her on.

In Dörfli everybody called to her, even more clamorously than before, all asking after Heidi. They had known Dete all her life, and knew Heidi's history, and longed to know what had happened to the child.

"Where is she?" they shouted from the windows. "Where's Heidi?" they called from the doorways. "What have you done with the little one, Dete?"

And Dete shouted back, more and more impatiently, "She's with the Alm Uncle! She's up on the mountain with the Alm Uncle, I tell you!"

"How could you do such a thing?" the women exclaimed.

Dete hurried on, feeling more uncomfortable than ever, their words pricking at her conscience.

"Poor little thing!" they muttered to each other. "To think of that helpless child being left up there."

Dete ran on as quickly as possible, the women's last words, "*Poor little thing!*" ringing in her ears. At last she was out of earshot and began to feel easier about what she had done.

But then she remembered her mother's words on her deathbed, asking her to take care of the child. "I can do more for Heidi when I've earned some money," Dete muttered. And she walked on, relieved to be leaving Dörfli behind her, and all the old friends who would question her too closely and try to make her change her mind. "I'm going into service with a good family," Dete told herself. "It's all for the best."

Chapter Two

At Grandfather's

After Dete had left, the old man sat down on his bench again. He blew out great clouds of smoke from his pipe, while staring at the ground in silence.

Heidi looked around in delight. She discovered the goat stall and peered in. Finding it empty, she carried on with her exploring. At last she went behind the hut and came to the old pines.

The wind was sighing and moaning in the branches, and the treetops swayed backwards and forwards. Heidi stood listening for a while, but the wind lulled, and she carried on round the hut until she came to her grandfather again. She stood in front of him, feet planted in the ground, hands clasped behind her back. After a few moments he raised his head and met her gaze.

"What do you want to do now?" he asked, as Heidi continued to stare at him.

"I want to see inside your hut," said Heidi.

"Well, take up your bundle, and follow me," said Grandfather, rising from the bench.

"I don't need my bundle any more," replied Heidi.

He turned at these words and looked at her sharply. Heidi's dark eyes were dancing with excitement, longing to peek inside the hut.

"She doesn't look like a fool..." he said to himself. "Why don't you think you need your things any more?" he asked out loud.

"I want to go about like the goats, barefoot and free," said Heidi. "They have such light little legs."

"Well, you can do that," replied Grandfather, gruffly. "But bring in the bundle all the same," he ordered. "We'll put it in the cupboard."

She picked up the bundle as he asked, then he opened the door and they went inside. There was just one large room, which made up the whole of the hut. In the middle stood a table, with a chair beside it. Grandfather's bed was in one corner, while in another a large kettle hung over a hearth. Grandfather went over to a large door in the wall opposite, which opened into a cupboard. In it hung his clothes, and there were shelves too, one stacked with his shirts, socks and handkerchiefs, another with cups, plates, saucers and glasses. On the top shelf was smoked meat, cheese and a round loaf of bread. The cupboard held everything Grandfather needed, and everything he owned.

Heidi stepped up with her bundle and stuffed it behind her grandfather's things, as far out of sight as possible. Then she looked carefully about the room. "Where shall I sleep, Grandfather?" she asked.

"Wherever you like," he replied.

His answer pleased her, and Heidi ran about the room, searching every corner, to find the best possible place. Opposite Grandfather's bed she found a ladder. Clambering up it, Heidi discovered a hayloft, strewn with fresh, sweet-smelling hay. There was a round window, and looking out, Heidi could see far, far away into the valley.

"Oh, I want to sleep here! It's so beautiful," she cried. "Come up, Grandfather! Come up, and see how beautiful it is."

"I know all about it," he answered from below.

"I'm making my bed here," said Heidi again, while she worked busily away, "but I'll need a sheet. Could you come up and bring me one?"

"All right," said Grandfather. He went to the cupboard, searched about, and at last pulled out a long, coarse linen cloth.

He came up the ladder with it and found Heidi had already made herself a little mattress out of hay, with another heap piled high for a pillow. She had arranged it all so she could lie in bed and gaze out the window at the valley.

"That's right," said the old man. "But it'll need to be thicker than that." And he took more hay and piled up the bed until it was twice as thick as before. "Now you won't feel the floor through the hay," said Grandfather. "Bring me the sheet," he added.

Heidi seized the sheet but it was so heavy she could hardly carry it. Together, they spread it over the hay, where it stopped the prickly hay stalks from poking through. The sheet was too long for such a small bed, so Heidi tucked it under as well. Then she stood admiring it for a long time. "We've forgotten one thing, Grandfather," she said at last.

"What's that?"

"A blanket! I'll need something to cover me when I'm lying on my sheet."

"Do you think so?" said Grandfather. "I'm not sure I have one."

"It doesn't matter," said Heidi. "I can easily cover myself with hay." She ran to fetch some, but Grandfather stopped her.

"Wait a moment," he said. He climbed down the ladder and went over to his bed. Then, climbing up again, he gave her a heavy blanket. "There! That's better than hay, isn't it?"

Heidi tried hard to spread out the blanket, but it was too heavy for her, so Grandfather began to help. The blanket was soon arranged over the bed and Heidi was entranced. "This is a beautiful blanket, and a perfect bed!" she said. "I wish it were bedtime, Grandfather, so that I could get into it."

"I think we should have something to eat first. What do you

think?" he asked.

Heidi had been so interested in her bed, she had forgotten everything else. Suddenly, she remembered how hungry she was. She'd eaten nothing since breakfast, which had only consisted of a piece of bread and a little weak coffee. Since then, she'd made the long journey up the mountain. "Oh yes," she said to Grandfather, "I think so too!"

"Let's go down then, since we agree," he said, and followed Heidi down the ladder. He went over to the fireplace, removed the big kettle and hung a small pot in its place, on the chain. Then he seated himself on the three-legged stool and blew on the fire until it was glowing and little flames danced in the grate. As the pot began to simmer, he put a large piece of cheese on a long iron fork and held it over the fire, slowly turning it round and round until it was golden yellow all over.

At first Heidi sat watching him, then she suddenly darted away towards the cupboard, before rushing back to the table. She did this again and again. When her grandfather brought the steaming pot and the toasted cheese to the table he found it was already laid, with the round loaf, two plates, two knives, all neatly arranged. Heidi had noticed them in the cupboard and knew they'd be needed for the meal.

"I'm glad you can think of things for yourself," said Grandfather, putting the cheese on the bread. "But there's something missing."

Heidi looked at the steaming pot again, and went back to the cupboard. She could only see one mug there, but then at the back, she spotted another. She quickly picked up both mugs and brought them over to the table.

"That's right. You're very helpful. But where are you going to sit?" Grandfather was sitting on the only high stool in the hut, but like an arrow, Heidi dashed over to the fireplace and brought over the little three-legged stool. She settled herself down on it.

"Well, you have a seat, at least," said Grandfather, "but it's rather low down. "

He stood up, filled the mug with milk and set it on his own

high stool. Then he drew it up to Heidi, so she had a table to herself. He perched on the corner of the table and picked up his plate. "Now we can begin our meal," he said.

Heidi seized her mug and drank without stopping. It was as if all the thirst of her journey had risen up at once. Then she drew a long breath, for in her eagerness to drink she hadn't stopped to breathe, and set down her mug.

"Does the milk taste good?" asked Grandfather.

"The best I've ever had," Heidi replied.

"Then you'd better have some more," said Grandfather, and he filled her mug to the brim. By now, Heidi had started on her bread, which was spread thickly with melted cheese. It tasted delicious. Every now and then she took a sip of her milk, and sat there feeling perfectly content.

When they'd finished eating, Grandfather went out to the goat stall. Heidi followed and watched him carefully as he swept the floor, then spread fresh straw on the ground for the goats to sleep on. Next, Grandfather went to the workshop next door and began to carve four round sticks, followed by a round board. He bored four holes in the board and stuck the sticks in. When he had finished, Heidi saw that he had made a stool just like his own, only higher. She watched him in silent amazement.

"What do you call this, Heidi?" asked Grandfather.

"That is my stool, because it's so high. You've made it so quickly!" she said.

"She's quick to notice things. She's observant," the old man remarked to himself as he moved round the hut with his hammer, checking to see what needed fixing. He drove a nail in here, tightened a screw there, constantly finding something to do, or to mend. Heidi followed him step by step, watching everything that he did. She was fascinated by everything. It was all so new to her.

At last the evening drew in. The wind began to sigh through the old trees. As it blew harder, all the branches swayed to and fro. The sound of the wind in the trees made Heidi so happy she could feel it in her heart. She ran out under the pines and leaped beneath their branches, jumping to catch them and laughing as the wind lifted them away from her again.

Her grandfather stood in the doorway and watched her leaping about in the dusk.

Suddenly, a shrill whistle cut through the air. Heidi stopped her jumping, and Grandfather came outside. Then Heidi saw a stream of goats coming down the mountain, one after the other, Peter walking in their midst.

With a joyful cry, Heidi ran towards them, stopping to greet all the goats she had made friends with that morning.

When they reached the hut, two beautiful, slender goats, one white and one brown, came out of the herd. They trotted up to Grandfather and licked his hands, for he gave them a little salt every evening to welcome them home. Peter went on his way with the rest of the herd, disappearing down the mountain, while Heidi gently patted the goats, one after the other.

"Are they ours, Grandfather? Are they really?" she asked excitedly. "Do they go into our stall? Will they always stay here with us?" Heidi poured out her questions, hardly giving Grandfather time to reply, other than to say, "Yes, yes, child," now and then.

When the goats had licked up all the salt, Grandfather said, "Run in and fetch your little mug and the bread." Heidi soon returned with them, and waited while Grandfather milked the white goat. He filled Heidi's mug with the fresh milk and cut a slice of bread for her. "Now eat your supper and then go to bed," he said. "Dete left another bundle for you. It's in the cupboard. You'll find your nightgown and anything else you may need. I must put the goats to bed now, so good night and sleep well."

"Good night, Grandfather, good night." As Grandfather disappeared round the corner with the goats, Heidi ran after him. "Oh, and what are their names?" she asked.

"The white one is called Little Swan, and the brown one is called Little Bear."

"Good night, Little Swan! Good night, Little Bear!" Heidi called as the goats trotted into their stall.

Then Heidi sat down on the bench to eat her bread and drink her milk. The wind was so strong that it almost blew her off her seat, so she ate as fast as she could, then went back into the hut. She climbed up the ladder to her bed and, in no time at all, was fast asleep, as if she were tucked up in the finest bed in the world.

Before it was dark, her grandfather came to bed too, as he always woke with the sun, which came up early over the mountains in summer. But as the night wore on, the wind grew so strong it shook the hut. The beams creaked and groaned, wild howls and sighs came down the chimney and outside, the old pines thrashed their branches in the fierce gusts.

"The child may be afraid," thought Grandfather, waking to the sound of the wind. He climbed up the ladder to Heidi's bed, just as the moon came out from behind the scudding clouds.

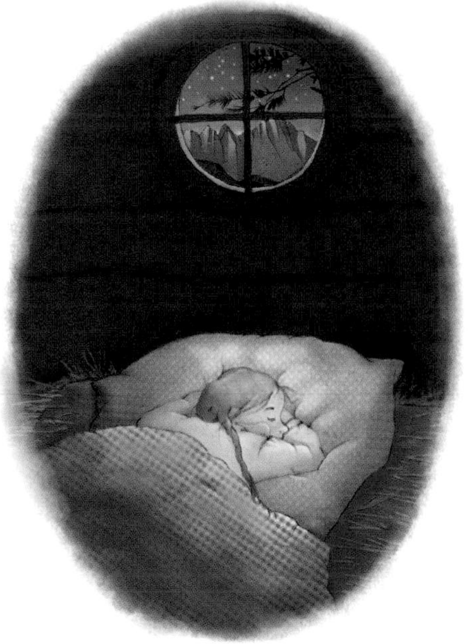

Its beams fell through the round window onto Heidi's bed, casting its glow on her round rosy cheeks and her smiling face. She looked as if she were dreaming of pleasant things.

The old man stood looking at Heidi as long as the moon shone. Then as the clouds darkened the room, he went down the ladder and back to bed.

Chapter Three

In the pasture

Early the next morning, Heidi was woken by a shrill whistle. As she opened her eyes a yellow sunbeam streaked in through her window, turning all the hay in the loft to gold. For a moment, she looked around in wonder, unable to remember where she was. Then she heard her grandfather's deep voice outside, and it all came back to her. She jumped up, quickly got dressed, raced down the ladder and out of the door.

Goat Peter was standing outside with his flock, and Grandfather was bringing out Little Swan and Little Bear from the stall to join them.

"Good morning!" Heidi called out to them all.

"Would you like to go with Peter and the goats to the

pasture?" asked Grandfather.

Heidi nodded vigorously.

"First you must wash and make yourself clean," said Grandfather, "or the sun will laugh at you, if he sees you all dirty and black. Look – everything is ready for you." He pointed to a big tub of water by the door. Heidi leaned over it and splashed and rubbed herself until she was clean. While she was washing, her grandfather went back into the hut, and soon called out to Peter, "Come here, Goat General, and bring your knapsack."

Peter obeyed in surprise, and opened his bag, revealing his small lunch.

"Wider, wider," said Grandfather. Peter's eyes grew rounder and rounder, as Grandfather put in a piece of bread and another piece of cheese, twice as big as Peter's.

"I'll put in Heidi's mug too. Fill it twice for her at lunchtime, as she can't drink milk straight from the goats as you do. And make sure you bring Heidi back with you in the evening. Mind you look after her too, and see that she doesn't fall off the cliffs."

Heidi came running in. "The sun won't laugh at me now, will it, Grandfather?" she asked. She had rubbed herself so hard with the towel that she was as red as a lobster. He chuckled.

"No there's nothing to laugh at now," he said. "But do you know what? When you come home this evening you have to go into the tub like a fish. If you go barefoot like the goats, you get dirty feet. Now get going, the pair of you."

Heidi was soon ready, and off they went, climbing up the Alm. The wind had swept all clouds from the sky, leaving it a wonderful wash of blue. Blue and yellow flowers sparkled among the grasses, their wide-open petals soaking up the sun.

Heidi rushed about, wild with excitement. She bent down to look at red cowslips, blue gentians and yellow rockroses, which seemed to laugh and nod in the sunlight. She was so absorbed by the flowers, that she forgot all about Peter and the goats. She ran about gathering great handfuls of flowers and stuffed them all in her apron. She had decided to take them home and scatter them over the hay in her bedroom, so it would look just like the Alm.

Poor Peter had to be constantly alert, watching for Heidi and the goats, which went their own way too, leaping this way and that on the mountainside. He had to whistle and shout and swing his stick to bring together all the wanderers.

"Where are you, Heidi?" he called out, rather angrily.

"Here," came back the reply.

But Peter couldn't see her anywhere, for Heidi was sitting among the bushes, where the ground was covered in prune flowers. Heidi sat taking long, deep breaths of their scent. She thought she had never breathed anything so perfectly delicious.

"Come here now," shouted Peter. "I don't want you falling over any cliffs. Your grandfather has forbidden it."

"Where are the cliffs?" Heidi called back, still not moving from her sweet-smelling spot.

"Up there! Right above us," said Peter. "Come along. We still have a long way to climb. Can you hear that screaming sound? That's the old eagle, who sits on the highest cliff."

Hearing this, Heidi jumped up and ran towards Peter, with her apron full of flowers.

"That's enough flowers," said Peter, as they began climbing again. "If you pick all the flowers today there won't be any left for tomorrow."

Heidi saw the sense in this and kept beside Peter now. So did the goats, for they could smell the tasty green leaves on the pasture above, and pushed forward without pausing, anxious to reach them.

Peter usually stopped for the day at the foot of a rocky mountain peak, where the pasturelands stretched out before them. On the steep slopes above, bushes and stunted pines grew out of the rocks, and high above them the soaring mountain peaks thrust up into the sky. The pastures themselves fell away in sheer precipices to the valley below.

When they reached his usual place, Peter took off his knapsack and placed it carefully in a little hollow. He knew what the wind was like up here, and didn't want to see his precious belongings sent rolling down the mountain by a sudden gust. Then he stretched himself out on the sunny ground to rest.

Heidi tucked her apron into the same hollow, first rolling up the flowers inside for safekeeping. Then she sat down beside Peter, and looked around her. Below, the valley lay in the full glow of the morning sun, and beyond she could see a huge, white snow-covered mountain that reached upwards until it seemed to touch the sky. To the left was a rocky mountain with jagged twin peaks. Heidi felt as if the pinnacles were looking down at her solemnly. She sat there as still as a mouse, looking around her. All was quiet. Only a light, soft breeze stirred the harebells and yellow rockroses that nodded on their slender stalks. Peter had fallen asleep and the goats were climbing among the bushes.

Heidi had never been so happy in all her life. She drank in the golden sunlight, the fresh air, the sweet scent of the flowers, and wished she could stay like this forever.

Time passed. Heidi gazed so long at the rocks above her that she began to see how they looked like faces, and were returning her gaze like old friends.

Suddenly she heard a sharp scream above her. Looking up, she saw a huge bird circling overhead. It soared through the air on widespread wings, going round and round in great sweeps. It screamed again, loudly and piercingly, over Heidi's head.

"Peter! Peter! Wake up!" cried Heidi. "The eagle is here! Look, look!"

Peter woke and together they gazed at the bird, which rose higher and higher, disappearing at last over the high rocks.

"Where is he now?" asked Heidi, who had watched the bird with breathless interest.

"In his nest up there."

"Oh, how beautiful to live all the way up there! But why does he scream so?"

"Because he must."

"Let's climb up and see his home," suggested Heidi.

"Oh no we won't!" said Peter. "Even the goats aren't able to climb up there."

Then Peter began to whistle and call so loudly that Heidi didn't know what was happening, until the goats came running and jumping towards them. Soon, they were all gathered on the green field. Some nibbled at the sweet grass, others ran about, while some stood opposite each other, a little way apart, and butted each other with their horns. Springing to her feet, Heidi ran to join them.

While Heidi skipped about with the goats, Peter fetched his knapsack, and arranged the parcels of food in a square on the grass, the big ones on Heidi's side, and the little ones on his. Then he filled the mug with fresh milk from Little Swan and placed it in the middle of the square.

"Time for lunch," called Peter, sitting down and beginning to eat. But Heidi didn't come as quickly as the goats did when he called. She was so busy leaping around with her new playmates she didn't notice anything else. Peter yelled until the cliffs echoed with his voice, until finally she saw the picnic all laid out, and came hopping over.

"Stop hopping about. It's lunchtime. Sit down and eat," ordered Peter.

Heidi drank the milk first, and when she had finished, Peter got up and filled her mug again. Heidi broke off some of her bread, and then handed the rest to Peter, who had already finished his food. She also gave him her big lump of cheese. "You have it all," she said to him. "I've had enough."

Peter stared at Heidi in astonishment. Never in his life had he been able to say that, or had anything to give away. He hesitated for a moment, unable to believe she meant it. But Heidi held out the food to him again, and when he didn't take it, she finally put it down on his knee.

When he saw that she was serious, he gave her a nod as a thank you and began to enjoy his feast. While he ate, Heidi watched the flock.

"What are all their names, Peter?"

Peter didn't know a great deal, but he could reel off the goats' names with ease. He named one after the other, pointing at each with his finger as he spoke. Heidi listened with rapt attention, studying them carefully, noticing their differences, until she could name them all too.

There was one called Bullfinch, who had very big horns, and was always trying to butt the others, and a small one called Goldfinch, who was the only one brave enough to fight back.

Then there was little white Snowflake, who kept bleating in

a sad voice, so that Heidi ran to her and put her arms around her neck, trying to comfort her. "What is it, Snowflake?" she asked. "Why do you call like that?" The little goat nuzzled Heidi trustingly and quitened down.

"It's because her mother's not with her," Peter called back. "She was sold at market the day before yesterday, so doesn't come up the mountain any more."

"Where's her grandmother? Or her grandfather?" asked Heidi.

"She doesn't have one," replied Peter.

"Oh you poor little Snowflake!" cried Heidi, hugging the goat to her. "But don't cry like that. I'll come up here every day with you, so you won't be alone any more."

As Peter finished his dinner, the goats began to climb towards the bushes again, each in its own way. Some sprang lightly over the rocks, while others kept their noses to the ground, searching for the next mouthful. Little Swan and Little Bear climbed nimbly, always avoiding Bullfinch, whom they treated with scorn. Heidi stood with her hands behind her back, observing them all.

"Peter," she announced at last, as he lay stretched out on the ground again. "Little Swan and Little Bear are the prettiest of them all."

"I know," said Peter, lazily. "The Alm Uncle washes and combs them. He gives them salt and keeps them in the cleanest stall."

No sooner had he finished speaking, than he was on his feet, leaping after the goats. Heidi dashed after him. She knew something must have happened and didn't want to be left behind.

Peter ran through the flock and up the side of the Alp, where the rocks rose steeply above him, and where a heedless goat could easily fall and break its legs. He'd caught sight of Goldfinch, an inquisitive little goat, straying towards the edge of a cliff. He scrambled after her, but as he reached out to seize her, he tripped and fell, catching only her leg as he came crashing down. He held fast, even as she bleated in surprise and anger, furious she couldn't carry on her journey.

"Heidi!" Peter called. "Help! Over here!" He couldn't get up without letting go of the goat, and was almost pulling her leg off, she was so determined to go forward. Heidi rushed over to him and realized at once what was happening. She quickly pulled up some sweet-smelling leaves and held them under Goldfinch's nose.

"Come here, little goat," she said soothingly. "Come here, Goldfinch, be good. You don't want to fall down there and hurt yourself."

The goat turned quickly and began to nibble on the leaves Heidi held out, now looking perfectly content.

Stumbling to his feet, Peter seized some string from his pocket and attached it to her collar as a lead. Then he and Heidi led the wanderer back down the slope to join the rest of the flock.

Once Goldfinch was safely on the pastures again, Peter raised his stick. Goldfinch drew back in alarm, and Heidi gasped in horror as she saw he was about to strike the little goat.

"No, Peter, no!" she screamed out. "You mustn't hit her. Can't you see how frightened she is?"

"She deserves it," said Peter angrily, raising his stick again.

But Heidi seized him by the arm. "No!" she cried again. "You mustn't touch her!"

Peter stared in surprise at Heidi, at her flashing eyes and commanding tone. He dropped his arm.

"Fine," he said. "I won't hit her. As long as you give me some of your cheese again tomorrow." He felt he should have something to console him after his fright.

"You can have it all, tomorrow and every day after that," Heidi assured him. "And I'll give you a big piece of bread too. But you must promise me not to hit Goldfinch, or Snowflake, or any of the other goats."

"It's all the same to me," said Peter, which was his way of making a promise, and he untied Goldfinch's lead and let her go. She quickly sprang away and raced off to join the other goats.

The day had passed, almost unnoticed by Heidi, and now the sun was begining to sink behind the mountain. She leaned back against a tree, gazing at the harebells and rockroses, noticing how the grass became golden and the rocks began to shimmer and flash in the glow of the fading sun.

A moment later, she cried out, "Peter, Peter! All the mountains are on fire! Everything's burning – even the snowy peak over there, and the sky... Look, look! The highest peak is glowing. What a beautiful fire! Now it has reached the eagle's nest..."

"It's always like that in the evening, but there's no fire," said Peter calmly.

"What is it, then?" asked Heidi, running about to take in the view. She wanted to see it from all sides, it looked so beautiful. "What is it, Peter?" she asked again.

"It just happens," he said.

"Look again!" she cried. "Everything has turned red as roses. Even the snow on those cliff tops. What are they called?"

"Mountains have no names," answered Peter.

"Oh, the lovely, rosy snow! But now they are growing pale... the fire's gone out... it's all gone, Peter." And Heidi threw herself on the ground looking as if it were the end of the world.

"It'll be the same again tomorrow," said Peter. "Now follow me. It's time to go back." He whistled the herd together, and they set out for home.

"Will it be the same every time we go to the pasture?" asked Heidi, longing for reassurance.

"Mostly," said Peter.

"But will it be the same tomorrow?"

"Yes, it'll be the same tomorrow," he assured her.

Heidi was quiet again and hardly spoke a word all the way down the Alm, she had so much to think about. At last the Alm hut came into view, and she could see her grandfather sitting under the pines, waiting for them.

"Grandfather!" she called, running towards him, with Little Swan and Little Bear at her heels.

"Come again tomorrow," said Peter, going on his way. "Good night, Heidi."

Heidi ran back to say goodbye, promising to go with him the next day. Then she hugged Snowflake one last time. "Sleep well," she whispered to the little goat. "And remember I'll be with you tomorrow and you're not to cry anymore."

Snowflake looked back at Heidi gratefully and scampered after the herd.

Then Heidi came back through the pine trees to her grandfather. "Oh!" she told him. "It was so beautiful! All the flowers... Oh, look what I've brought!" And opening her apron, she shook out all the flowers she had gathered. But they were like dry bits of hay, their petals faded and torn.

"What's the matter with them?" cried Heidi. "They weren't

like that this morning."

"They like to be in the sun, not shut up in an apron," replied Grandfather.

"Then I will never pick any more," said Heidi, sadly. "But, Grandfather, why did the eagle cry?"

"You get into the tub while I put the goats in the stall and get your milk. Then we'll go inside and I'll tell you over supper."

Later, when Heidi was sitting on her high stool, with her milk, she repeated her question. "Why does the eagle keep screaming and crying at us?"

"He's mocking the people who live down below in the villages, all crammed together making each other cross," said Grandfather. "He's calling, 'You'd all feel much better if you had more space and lived up here like me.'"

"Why don't the mountains have names, Grandfather?" she asked next.

"They do have names," he replied. "If you can describe one so I recognize it, I'll tell you what it's called."

So Heidi described the craggy mountain with two high peaks, and Grandfather said, "I know it. It's called Falknis. Did you see any more?"

Then Heidi described the one with the big snowfield, and how it had suddenly glowed like fire, then turned rose red, and had at last grown pale again.

"I recognize that one too," said Grandfather. "That one's

called Scesaplana."

"And where does the fire come from?" Heidi asked. "Peter couldn't tell me."

"It's the sun's way of saying good night to the mountains," Grandfather replied. "He casts his most beautiful beams across them, so they won't forget he's coming back again in the morning."

This pleased Heidi. Now she could hardly wait for tomorrow, when she could go up to the pasture again and see the sun say good night to the mountains. But first she had to go to sleep. She lay down in her little hay bed again, and slept the whole night through, dreaming of rose-red mountains with a little white goat bounding happily across them.

Chapter Four

At Grandmother's

The next morning was bright and sunny again, and Heidi went with Peter and the goats, climbing up to the mountain pastures. All through that summer, Heidi went with Peter, growing strong and brown under the summer sun. She was as merry as a bird in the treetops.

As the summer drew to a close, the wind blew harder over the mountains. Sometimes her grandfather would say, "You must stay at home today, Heidi. Someone as little as you might easily be blown down the mountain by the wind."

When Peter heard those words, he frowned and trudged on alone. He was so lonely and bored without Heidi, he didn't know what to do with himself. He didn't have his extra bread and cheese any more and the goats were more unruly without her. They wouldn't go on as before, but scattered in every direction, almost as if they were looking for her. Heidi, however, was never unhappy as there was always something new to enjoy. She loved being up on the meadow with Peter and the goats, but Grandfather's sawing and hammering entertained her too. This was the time of year he made round goats' cheese and it was fascinating watching him roll up his sleeves and mix the cheese by hand. But, best of all, were the three old pines behind the hut. On windy days, Heidi couldn't get enough of the sight and sound of them waving and sighing in the wind.

As the warmth of the sun faded, Heidi still longed to go out. She would stand under the pine trees, watching the wind swaying the branches. Sometimes it blew so strongly she was blown about herself, like a leaf in a gale.

As the months passed, it turned colder still. Peter would arrive blowing on his fingers to keep them warm, and then one day, he didn't come at all. There had been a deep snowfall in the night, and in the morning the whole Alm was white, without a green leaf to be seen. Heidi sat inside the hut looking through the tiny window. She watched thick snowflakes fill the air, until the snow was as high as the windowsill. Then it was higher still, so they couldn't open the window at all.

Heidi loved being safe and snug inside the hut. She ran from one window to the next to look at the view. She longed for the snow to pile up around them, so they'd be buried inside and have to light the lamp in the daytime.

But the snow never covered them completely. The next day, the snow stopped falling and Grandfather went out with his shovel to make a path around the house. He sprayed shovelfuls of snow in the air, and where it landed, it made little mountains all around the hut.

Then Heidi and her grandfather sat down for lunch together. Suddenly, there was a loud knock on the door, and someone struggled and kicked at it. At last it was flung open, and there stood Peter, covered from head to toe in snow. It clung to him in frozen clumps, sticking to his clothes and his hair. He had been forced to walk through huge snowdrifts, but he'd bravely kept going so that he could see Heidi again. A whole week had been too long without her.

"Good afternoon," he said, then without another word, he came and stood as near to the fire as possible. He was smiling from ear to ear, he was so pleased to be there. Heidi stared at him in wonder. The fire was beginning to melt the snow that covered him, and he looked more like a waterfall than Peter.

"Well, General," said the old man. "How are you getting on now that you have no army of goats? You must be chewing your pencil, I suppose."

"Why is he chewing a pencil?" asked Heidi curiously.

"He has to go to school in the winter," explained Grandfather.

"He has to learn to read and write, which is difficult, and it helps to chew on a pencil sometimes. Isn't that so?"

"Yes, it's true," said Peter.

Now Heidi began to ask question after question. She wanted to know what happened at school, what he saw and what he did there. Peter tried to keep up with her questions, but he was never very quick with his words. By the time Heidi had finished, the snow had thawed from his clothes and he was dry once more.

The old man watched them in silence, only the occasional flicker of an amused smile to show he was listening.

"Now, General," he said, when Heidi paused for a moment. "You've been under fire and I expect you need some food." As he spoke, he went to the cupboard and brought what was needed for supper, while Heidi set the table.

There was a new bench nailed against the wall, so they could all sit comfortably around the table. Since Heidi had moved in, the hut looked much less bare. It was full of seats for two people, as Heidi liked to follow her grandfather around, to watch what he was doing and sit beside him.

Peter's eyes grew huge and round as he watched the Alm Uncle put a huge piece of dried meat on a thick slice of bread for him. It was a long time since he'd had such a good meal. As soon as they'd finished eating Peter got ready to go, for it was growing dark outside.

"Good night," Peter said, standing in the doorway. Then,

turning back again, he added, "I'll come again on Sunday. And you should come and visit Grandmother. She said so."

Heidi was very excited by the idea of visiting Peter's grandmother. She could think of nothing else. First thing the next morning she said, "I'm off to see Grandmother. She's expecting me."

"There's far too much snow," replied her grandfather.

But Heidi was not to be put off so easily. Grandmother had asked her to come, so she must go. She asked Grandfather at least five or six times a day. "I must go," she would say, "Grandmother is expecting me."

On the fourth day, everything still snapped and crackled in the cold. But as Heidi sat on her high stool at lunch, she saw the sun shining beautifully on the frozen snow outside. "Today I *will* visit Grandmother," she said, "or she'll think I'm not coming."

Suddenly Grandfather rose from the table. He went into the loft, and brought down Heidi's blanket. "Well then, let's go!" he said.

Heidi ran out after him into the glistening snow. The old pine trees were quiet now, with the white snow lying heavily on their branches. They sparkled and glittered in the sunlight. "Look, Grandfather!" said Heidi. "The trees are all silver and gold."

Grandfather appeared from the workshop, with a big toboggan. He beckoned to Heidi, sat down on the toboggan and pulled Heidi onto his lap. Then he wrapped her in the blanket until she

The toboggan shot down the Alm, flying across the snow so fast that Heidi shouted with excitement.

was warm and snug. He held her tightly in his arms and with a great shove of his feet, they were off. The toboggan shot down the Alm, flying across the snow so fast that Heidi shouted with excitement.

Grandfather steered it all the way to Goat Peter's door. He placed Heidi on the ground, unwrapped her from the blanket and gestured for her to go in.

"Come back out again as soon as it begins to grow dark, mind," he said, "and start for home." Then, turning back, he began to climb the mountain, pulling the toboggan behind him.

Heidi opened the door, and entered a small room. It looked very dark inside. She could just make out a hearth, and some plates and dishes on the shelves. As her eyes grew accustomed to the dim light, she realized it was, in fact, a little kitchen. She opened another door, and came into another little room. This house wasn't a mountain hut like the Alm Uncle's, with one large room and a hayloft above, but a very old dwelling, where everything was small and narrow and uncomfortable.

Stepping into the room, Heidi bumped straight into a table. A woman was sitting in front of it, mending trousers – Peter's trousers. Heidi recognized them at once.

In the corner, a bent little old woman was sitting at a spinning wheel. Heidi knew instantly who she was. "Good day Grandmother," she said, going straight over to her. "I've come to see you at last. Did you think I was never going to come?"

Grandmother raised her head and reached out, feeling for Heidi's hand, which she took in her own. She held it thoughtfully for a while. "Are you the child who lives with the Alm Uncle?" she asked. "Are you Heidi?"

"Yes, I am Heidi. I've just come down the mountain with Grandfather. On the toboggan!"

"Is that really possible? And yet you have such nice warm hands. Tell me, Brigitte, did the Alm Uncle bring the child himself?"

Peter's mother, who had been mending clothes, stood up now, and looked at Heidi curiously.

"I don't know if the Alm Uncle brought her himself," she said. "I can't believe it though. The child must be confused."

Heidi looked fixedly at the woman. "I know exactly who wrapped me in a blanket and brought me down on the toboggan in his arms. It was Grandfather."

"Then it must be true, what Peter has been telling us all summer," said Grandmother. "And we all thought he was mistaken. Who would have believed it! I didn't think a child could last three weeks up there. How does she look, Brigitte?"

"She's slim like her mother was," replied Brigitte. "But she has the same dark eyes and thick hair as her father, and the old man up there."

While Brigitte and Grandmother were talking, Heidi had been inspecting the little room, taking in every detail. "Look at the shutter, Grandmother," she said now. "It's swinging about in the wind. Grandfather could nail it in for you, to hold it fast. Otherwise it will break one of your panes. See how it swings!"

"I can't see it," said Grandmother, "but I always hear it banging to and fro. And not just the shutter. Everything in this house creaks and groans when the wind blows, and we feel the wind too, blasting through the walls. In the night, when everyone else is asleep, I lie awake, anxious that the house will fall in on us, and that we'll all be killed. There's no one to help us. Peter doesn't know how to fix things."

"But why can't you see the shutter, Grandmother? It's just over there! Can't you see it swinging?"

"Oh, child, I can't see anything at all! Not the shutter, not anything," said Grandmother sadly.

"But what if I open all the shutters and you look out the window, where everything is white with snow? Won't you be able to see in the light?"

"Nothing will ever make me see again, neither snow nor sun. No light enters my eyes now."

Heidi began to cry. "Can't someone help you to see again?" she sobbed. "Isn't there anyone who can do it?"

Grandmother tried in vain to comfort her. Heidi hardly ever cried but when she did, she found it hard to stop. "Come here," Grandmother said at last, drawing Heidi towards her. "I have something to tell you. Even though I can't see anything, I can

listen, and that gives me huge pleasure. So come and sit down by me, and tell me things. What do you do up there on the Alm, and what does your grandfather do? I used to know him, but I haven't seen him, or heard about him for such a long time. Except from Peter, I suppose, but he never says very much."

"Oh!" cried Heidi, as an idea struck her, wiping away her tears with her sleeve. "I know what I'll do. I'll tell Grandfather all about you and he'll be able to make you see. And he'll mend your hut. He can do anything."

Grandmother didn't reply, and so Heidi began to describe her life with Grandfather. She told her how he could make all sorts of things, seats and stools and mangers for Little Swan and Little Bear, and a huge water tub to bathe in when summer came. And she told Grandmother how she watched him and how she hoped one day she would be able to make the same things herself.

Suddenly there was a stamping noise at the door, and their conversation was interrupted by Peter bursting into the room. He stared at Heidi with his big round eyes, then grinned at her as she greeted him.

"Have they let you out of school already?" asked Grandmother. "I can't think when an afternoon has passed so quickly. How was your reading today, Peterkin?"

"Just the same," replied Peter.

"Oh dear. I thought it might have improved a little by now. You'll be twelve in February," she added, with a little sigh.

"Why should it have improved by now?" asked Heidi.

"I only meant that perhaps he might have learned to read," said Grandmother. "I have an old prayer book up there on the shelf. There are beautiful hymns in it. I haven't heard them for such a long time, and I can't remember them any more. So I hoped that when Peterkin learned to read, he could sometimes read me a hymn. But it's no use. He can't learn. It's just too hard for him."

"I think I must light the lamp, Mother," said Brigitte, who had been working on Peter's trousers all this time. "It's quite dark, now. The afternoon has flown away without my knowing it."

"Oh, is it dark already?" asked Heidi, springing up from her chair. "Then I must go straight home." She took Grandmother's hand as she spoke, then said good night to Peter and his mother and went towards the door.

"Wait a moment. Wait, Heidi!" cried Grandmother, anxiously. "You mustn't go alone. Peter must go with you, won't you Peterkin? And do take care of her. Don't let her fall, or stand still, in case she gets frostbite. Has she got a thick shawl?"

"I don't have a shawl, but I won't be cold, Grandmother," said Heidi, and she was out of the house, running so quickly that Peter could hardly keep up with her.

"Run after her, Brigitte," called Grandmother, tremulously. "She'll freeze in that night air. Take my shawl with you and run."

Brigitte obeyed, but Peter and Heidi hadn't gone far up the mountain when they saw the Alm Uncle coming towards them. In a few great strides he was with them.

"Well done, Heidi," he said. "You've kept your promise and left before nightfall." He bent down and wrapped her carefully in the thick blanket, then picked her up in his arms and turned towards home.

Brigitte and Peter hurried back to their cottage, out of the cold winter air, to tell Grandmother what they had seen.

Grandmother listened to them in surprise. "I'm glad the Alm Uncle is so kind to Heidi. I do hope he'll let her come again. Her visit has done me so much good. She has a kind heart, that child, and how she chatters!" All evening, Grandmother kept saying, "If only she can come again. Now I have something to look forward to. I have something to make me happy."

Brigitte agreed with her mother, while Peter grinned from ear to ear. "I knew she'd do you good," he said. "I told you so."

Meanwhile, Heidi was chatting away to Grandfather from inside her blanket. But her voice couldn't reach him through the thick folds, she was so well wrapped up. "Wait until we get home, child," said Grandfather. "Then you can tell me all about it."

As soon as they reached the hut, Heidi threw off her blanket. "Tomorrow," she began in a rush, "we must take the hammer and the big nails and go down to Peter's hut, Grandfather. Their shutters bang about in the wind and we must mend them. And we need to put nails all over the house to fix things down, so it won't shake in the wind anymore."

"Must we, indeed?" said Grandfather. "And who told you that?"

"Nobody told me. I decided it for myself. The house is about to fall apart, and it makes Grandmother so nervous and afraid. She can't sleep there is so much noise, and she's worried the house will fall down on their heads. And oh! Did you know, Grandfather, she can't see, and no one can make it light for her again? But you can, can't you Grandfather? Only think how sad it must be, always to sit in the dark, and how awful it is for her! Tomorrow we'll go and help her, won't we, Grandfather?"

Heidi was clinging to her grandfather, and looking up at him, her eyes full of confidence. He looked at her for a long time in silence. "Yes," he said at last, "we'll fix up Grandmother's house, so it won't clatter and keep her awake. We can do that at least. We'll go tomorrow."

Heidi danced around the room. "Tomorrow we'll go!" she cried joyfully. "Tomorrow we'll go!"

Grandfather kept his promise. The next afternoon they took their toboggan and rode down the mountain again. "You go in," he said to Heidi, lifting her out by the front door. "And I'll go round the house with my hammer. Come out again in the evening."

Heidi had scarcely opened the door, and stepped into the room, when Grandmother called out from her seat in the corner. "Here comes Heidi!" she cried. She stopped her spinning and stretched out her arms towards her.

Heidi ran to her and, sitting as close to the old woman as possible, began chatting away about anything and everything, until her voice was drowned out by a pounding outside the hut.

"Oh goodness!" said Grandmother, starting to tremble, nearly overturning her spinning wheel in fright. "It's happening. What I've always dreaded is happening. The house is falling down."

Heidi gently took hold of her arm. "No, it's not, Grandmother," she said soothingly. "Don't be afraid. It's only Grandfather with his hammer. He's mending your house so you don't need to be frightened anymore."

"Is it really true?" asked Grandmother. "Did you hear that, Brigitte. Yes, that sound really is a hammer. Go out and ask the

Alm Uncle to come in for a moment, so I can thank him."

Brigitte ran outside, to find the Alm Uncle fixing the wooden slats to the walls. "Good evening, Uncle," she said. "My mother wants to thank you. We're so grateful that you're doing this for us. No one has ever been so kind to us before. Will you come in, so—"

"You've said quite enough," interrupted the old man. "I know what you think of me. Go back inside. I can work out what needs doing for myself."

Brigitte hurried back inside, cowed by the force of his will. Grandfather went on pounding and hammering around the house, then climbed the narrow steps to the roof, hammering until he'd used every nail he'd brought with him. By this time it was nearly dark, and as he came down to fetch his toboggan from behind the goat stall, he saw Heidi standing ready at the door. Grandfather picked her up in his arms, using one hand to drag the toboggan behind him.

"It's too cold for you to sit alone on the toboggan," he explained, as he trudged up the mountain. "Your blanket would fall off and you'd freeze with cold."

All through the winter, Heidi went to visit Grandmother, and the old woman felt as if happiness had come into her life again. Her days were no longer dark and joyless, with each one exactly the same as the next. Now there was always something to look forward to. Every morning she would listen out for the sound of

Heidi's footsteps, and when Heidi came in she would cry, "Oh! You've come again!"

And Heidi would sit by her and tell her everything she knew, so that time slipped by. When Heidi left, Grandmother always said, "How short the afternoon seemed, don't you think, Brigitte? And does she look well and strong?"

And Brigitte always answered, "She looks bright and rosy as an apple."

When Heidi knew for certain that no one could make Grandmother see again, she was filled with sorrow. But Grandmother told her that she felt the darkness much less when Heidi was with her, and so she came every fine winter's day, making her way down on the toboggan.

Without anything more being said, the Alm Uncle would come too, bringing his hammer and his tools. He spent his time pounding and mending until at last he had repaired the whole house. It no longer rattled at night to keep Grandmother awake. "I haven't had such comfortable nights in years," she told Heidi. "I'll always be grateful to your grandfather."

Chapter Five

Unexpected visitors

The winter passed quickly, and another happy summer, and now a second winter was nearing its end. Heidi was looking forward to spring, when the south wind would sweep through the pines and drive away the snow. Then the warm sun would summon the flowers on the pastures, and Heidi would be able to go up the mountain with Peter again, and spend her days as she loved best.

Heidi was seven now, and learning everything she could from Grandfather. She could take care of the goats, Little Swan and Little Bear. They ran at her heels and bleated with pleasure at the sound of her voice.

Twice during the winter, Peter had come with a message from the schoolmaster, asking the Alm Uncle to send Heidi to school.

She was more than old enough, but each time Grandfather had refused. "If the schoolmaster has anything to say to me," he told Peter, "he can come up the Alm and tell me to my face. I have no plans to send Heidi to school."

By March, the sun had begun to melt the snow. Heidi ran back and forth, from the house to the goat stall to the pines, telling Grandfather all about the green patch under the trees, and how much it was growing.

One morning, as Heidi was dashing out the door for the tenth time, she saw an old man standing in front of her. He was dressed all in black, gazing at her solemnly. Heidi nearly fell back in fright.

"Don't be afraid," said the old man, seeing her surprise. "I didn't mean to startle you. Come, let's shake hands. You must be Heidi. Where's your grandfather?"

"He's at the table, making wooden spoons," explained Heidi, and she opened the door wider to let him in.

It was the pastor, whom the Alm Uncle had known many years ago, when he had lived in Dörfli.

"Good morning, friend," said the pastor.

The Alm Uncle looked up in surprise. "Good morning!" he replied, immediately getting up from the table to fetch the pastor a stool. "Sit down, if you don't mind a hard seat."

"It's a long time since I last saw you," remarked the pastor.

"Likewise," replied the Alm Uncle.

"I came to speak to you about something," the pastor went on.

"I think you can probably guess what..." He stopped and looked towards Heidi, who was still standing in the doorway.

"You may go and see the goats, Heidi," said Grandfather. "Give them a little salt and stay there until I come."

As soon as Heidi had gone, the pastor began again. "That child ought to be in school. In fact, she should have been in school last year! The teacher asked for her to come and you never did anything about it."

"I'm not going to send her to school," was all the Alm Uncle said in reply. He folded his arms across his chest and looked stubbornly at the pastor.

The pastor could only stare back in astonishment. "Then what are you going to do about the child's education?"

"Nothing. She lives with the goats and the birds. She's happy. She'll learn no evil from them. She's safe here."

"But she's not a goat or a bird. She's a little girl. She may learn nothing evil from the animals around her, but she's not learning to read or write either. It's high time she began her education. I've come to warn you, so that you can think it over, and make your arrangements during the summer. Next winter, she must begin at school, and go every day."

"I won't do it," replied the Alm Uncle, unmoved.

"Haven't you listened to a word I've said? You are being obstinate and foolish," cried the pastor. "You've been about the world, and must have learned much. I thought that you had more sense than this."

"Well," replied the old man, his voice no longer calm. "Do you really think it would be a good idea for me to send a small child down the mountain in winter, in the snow and the wind? It would take her two hours to get down and then she would have to come up again every evening. It would be too much for an adult, let alone a child. Do you remember Heidi's mother, Adelheid, who was so delicate and fell into strange swoons? Do you want me to make Heidi unwell, by forcing her to do too much? If you do make me, I'm happy to go before a judge about it. Then we'll see what happens."

"You are right," replied the pastor in a more friendly tone. "It wouldn't be possible to send Heidi down to school from here. But I can see that you are fond of her, so do something for her sake that you should have done long ago. Come down to the village and live among people again. What sort of life do you lead up here, at odds with God and man? If anything should happen to you here in the winter, how could any of us help you? I don't even know how such a small child can get through the winter up here without freezing."

"I'll tell you! The child has young blood and warm clothes. I know where to get wood, and the best time to fetch it. You can look in my shed if you like. There is plenty of fuel there. The fire in my hearth never goes out, all winter long. It wouldn't suit me to live in the village. The people down there despise me, and I despise them. It's best for us all that we remain apart."

"It's not good for you," said the pastor. "And people don't think as badly of you as you think. Seek your peace with God, ask for his forgiveness in whatever way you need it. Then come back to Dörfli and see how differently the people treat you, and how happy you can be there."

The pastor stood up and held out his hand to the Alm Uncle. "I'll count on having you among us next winter. We are old friends, and I'd hate to have to force you. Give me your hand and promise you'll come back and live with us again, at peace with God and man."

The Alm Uncle gave his hand to the pastor. "I know you mean it kindly, but I'll not do as you wish," he said decisively. "I'll neither send Heidi to school, nor come to Dörfli."

"May God help you!" said the pastor sadly, and he went out the door and down the mountain.

After he left, the Alm Uncle was surly and curt. Heidi asked if they could go and see Grandmother. "Not today," her grandfather replied, and didn't speak again the whole day. The next morning, Heidi asked to go and see Grandmother again. "We'll see," was all he would say.

But before there was time to clear the table after dinner, another visitor arrived. This time it was Dete. She wore a fine hat with a feather, and a dress that swept up everything in its path. And in the Alm Uncle's mountain hut, there were quite a few things that lay in its path. The Alm Uncle looked at her from head to foot, but didn't say a word.

"Heidi looks very well," Dete exclaimed. "I hardly recognize her. You've obviously looked after her and cared for her." And then she went on talking for some time, without stopping. "I always meant to come for the child, of course, and take her back. I know it must have been difficult for you to look after her, but I never had a moment to come for her. But I'm here now as I've found such a brilliant situation for Heidi. I can hardly believe it! Such a piece of luck!"

Grandfather didn't respond, so Dete continued, "I've discovered there are some very rich relations of the family I work for, who own the grandest house in Frankfurt. They have only one daughter, who is unwell, and has to stay in a wheelchair all the time. She's almost always alone, with only her tutor for company, which must be very dull for her. The family want to find a companion for her, to live in the house. The housekeeper said they wanted a perfectly unspoiled little girl, quite out of the ordinary. As soon as I heard this, of course I thought of Heidi.

"I went to the housekeeper and told her about Heidi, and spoke so well of her, the housekeeper agreed at once that she is just what they are looking for. Who could have thought Heidi had such a future! When she lives with this family, she'll have everything the daughter has and you never know... the daughter is so delicate... If the family is left without a child, it might well be that—"

"Have you nearly finished?" interrupted Grandfather.

"Ha!" said Dete, tossing her head. "You're behaving as if I'd brought you the most commonplace piece of news. There's no one in the whole valley who wouldn't have been overjoyed to be told what I've just told you."

"Tell them, then," said the old man. "It doesn't interest me."

At these words, Dete went off like a rocket. "If that's your opinion, Uncle, I'll give you mine. Heidi is nearly eight years old, and knows nothing! You won't let her learn, or send her to school, or even to church. They told me all about it down in Dörfli. She is my only sister's child and I must be responsible for her. She has an opportunity now and she must take it. I'll not back down on this, I can tell you, and there's not a single person down in Dörfli who isn't on my side. And if you want to take this to court, you'd better think again. I can bring up things against you that you'd much rather were forgotten."

"Hold your tongue!" thundered the old man, his eyes flashing fire. "Take the child, and ruin her, but never bring her back here again! I don't want to see her with a feather in her hat or with words in her mouth such as you've used today." And he strode out of the hut.

"You've made Grandfather angry," said Heidi, her eyes fierce, her stare unfriendly.

"Oh, he'll be all right. Come along. Where are your clothes?"

"I'm not going," said Heidi.

"What did you say?" said Dete. Then changing her tone a little, she continued, half coaxingly, half angry. "Come, come, you don't know what you're talking about. It'll be much nicer in Frankfurt than you can imagine."

She went to the cupboard, took out Heidi's things and put them in her bag. "Come, now, get your hat. It doesn't look very nice, I must say, but it'll have to do. Put it on, and we'll be off."

"I'm not going," repeated Heidi.

"You're being as stupid and obstinate as the goats. You must have learned it from them. Think about it! You heard your grandfather just now, telling us never to come back. You saw how angry he was. He wants you to go with me. Don't make him even angrier. You have no idea how lovely it is in Frankfurt, or what you'll see there. And if you don't like it, you can come back here again, and by that time Grandfather will have calmed down. "

"Can I come home this evening?"

"Oh, just come on, will you? I said you can come back whenever you want. Today we go as far as Mayenfeld, and early tomorrow morning we'll get on the train. But if you want to come home, the train will take you back again in the blink of an eye. It's like flying."

Dete took Heidi's hand in hers, and they went down the mountain together.

It was too early in the year for Peter to take the goats to the pasture, so he was at school in Dörfli – or should have been. He often played truant for the day, as he couldn't see the point of school if he couldn't learn to read, and much preferred searching for firewood instead.

It happened that he was standing near his hut, with a big bundle of hazel sticks on his shoulder, as Heidi and Dete came down the mountain. "Where are you going?" he asked them.

"I have to go to Frankfurt with Aunt Dete," replied Heidi. "But I'll run in and see Grandmother first."

"No!" said Dete, anxiously holding Heidi by the hand, as Heidi struggled to reach the door. "There's no time to stop and talk. You can come back again and see her soon, but you must come with me now."

And she pulled Heidi along behind her, and didn't let go of her hand again. She was worried Heidi might decide not to go with her after all, or that Grandmother would persuade her to stay.

Peter burst into the hut, throwing his bundle of sticks down so hard on the table that everything trembled. Grandmother started from her spinning. "What's the matter?" she cried out. "What's happened, Peter?"

His mother, who had been sitting quietly at the table, almost flew into the air at the noise. "What is it, Peterkin?" she asked. "Why are you so angry?"

"Because she has taken Heidi away with her," cried Peter.

"Who? Who? Where, Peterkin?" cried Grandmother. Then in a moment she guessed what had happened, for Brigitte had told her earlier that she'd seen Dete going up the mountain to the Alm Uncle's. Trembling all over, the old woman opened the window. "Dete, Dete!" she called beseechingly. "Don't take the child away! Don't take Heidi away from us!"

Heidi and Dete were still within earshot, but at Grandmother's words, Dete only held Heidi more tightly and began to run.

"Grandmother is calling me," Heidi protested, trying to pull away. "Let me go to her."

"There's no time," snapped Dete, dragging Heidi along. "When we get to Frankfurt you'll like it so much you won't want to come back. But if you do, you could first find something there that Grandmother would like."

This idea pleased Heidi, and she stopped trying to turn back and began to run along with Dete. "What can I bring

Grandmother?" she asked, after a while.

"Something good to eat," suggested Dete. "Some beautiful, soft, white rolls perhaps. I expect she finds it hard to bite into the hard, black bread. That would be nice for her."

"Yes, yes! She always gives her bread to Peter, and says she can't manage it. I've often seen her do that. Let's go quickly, Aunt Dete, and perhaps we can get to Frankfurt today. Then I can come back straight away with the white rolls."

Now it was Heidi who urged her aunt along. She ran so quickly that Dete found it hard to follow with her bag. But she was glad to go quickly, for they were coming into Dörfli, and she didn't want to be flooded with more questions that might make Heidi change her mind.

They raced through the village, Heidi dragging her aunt by the hand. Dete was glad to think everyone would see that it was this way round.

People called out to her from their houses to stop. "I can't possibly!" Dete was pleased to reply. "Heidi is in such a hurry, and we still have far to go."

"Are you taking her with you?" "Are you running away from the Alm Uncle?" "It's a miracle the child is living!" "And she looks so well!" Questions and remarks bombarded her from all sides. Dete was relieved she could escape without answering, or offering explantions. She was thankful, too, that Heidi didn't say a word, but ran on as quickly as she could.

From that day on, the Alm Uncle looked more forbidding than ever. He didn't speak to anyone when he passed through Dörfli to sell his cheeses and buy his bread in the valley below. He looked so fierce, with his thick stick in his hand and his eyebrows joined together in a frown, that mothers would warn their children to keep their distance.

Everyone gossiped as he passed, agreeing how lucky Heidi was to have escaped from him, and how eager she had been to get away.

Only blind old Grandmother stood up for the Alm Uncle. She told everyone who came to her with wool to spin how kind and careful he had been with Heidi. She told them of all the afternoons he had spent mending the house. But most people remarked that Grandmother was so old she must have become confused, and that she was probably deaf now as well as blind.

The Alm Uncle never came to Goat Peter's home anymore, but he had mended the little house so thoroughly it could withstand the roar of the wind.

Grandmother's days passed slowly again, and she began each one with a sigh. "The days are so long and empty now," she said. "I wish I could hear Heidi's voice again before I die."

Chapter Six

All kinds of new things

In a grand house in Frankfurt, Mr. Sesemann's sickly daughter Clara was sitting in her wheelchair. She spent all day in it, being rolled from one room to another. At this moment she was in the study next to the large dining room. It was plain from all the bits and pieces lying around that she spent much of her time there. The study walls were lined with glass-fronted cabinets full of books. This was where Clara had her lessons.

Clara had a pale, thin face and gentle, blue eyes. At the moment these eyes were fixed on a wall clock, the hands of which seemed to be moving particularly slowly today. Clara was usually a very patient girl, but she suddenly asked, with a definite note of impatience, "Is it time yet, Miss Rottenmeyer?"

Miss Rottenmeyer was sitting very upright at a desk, busy with her embroidery. She wore a mysterious sort of cape with a large collar that gave her a solemn appearance, enhanced by the high, dome-shaped hat she wore on her head. For many years now, since the mistress of the house had died, Miss Rottenmeyer had been responsible for the housekeeping and the supervision of the servants. Mr. Sesemann was often away and entrusted her with the running of the household, with the condition that his daughter should be consulted about everything and nothing could be done against her wishes.

While Clara asked again whether it was time, downstairs a horsedrawn coach had arrived, and was depositing Dete and Heidi at the front door. As they climbed out, Dete asked Johann the coachman whether she would be permitted to disturb Miss Rottenmeyer so late in the day.

"That's not for me to decide," grumbled the coachman. "Ring for Sebastian. There's a bell in the corridor."

Dete did as she was told, and down the stairs came the servant. He had big, round buttons on his uniform, matched by a pair of big, round eyes in his face.

"I wanted to ask whether I may disturb Miss Rottenmeyer so late in the day," Dete repeated.

"That's not for me to decide," replied Sebastian. "Ring for Tinette using the other bell." With that, he disappeared.

Dete rang again. Next, the maid Tinette appeared with a

brilliant white cap perched on her head, and a scornful expression on her face. "What is it?" she asked from the top of the stairs.

Dete repeated her question. Tinette disappeared, but soon reappeared and called down, "They're expecting you."

Dete led Heidi up the stairs and followed Tinette into the study. She waited politely at the door holding Heidi tightly by the hand, as she wasn't sure what the girl might do in such unfamiliar surroundings.

Miss Rottenmeyer heaved herself slowly out of her chair and came closer to examine the new arrival. She didn't look too pleased. Heidi was wearing a simple cotton dress and an old, misshapen straw hat. She looked all around herself, gazing up at the towering hat on Miss Rottenmeyer's head with open wonder.

Miss Rottenmeyer looked searchingly at the child for a few minutes, and Heidi held her gaze the entire time. Then the lady said, "What is your name?"

"Heidi," was the reply.

"What? What? That can't be your Christian name. What name were you christened with?" asked Miss Rottenmeyer.

"I can't remember," replied Heidi.

"What an answer," remarked Miss Rottenmeyer, shaking her head. "Dete, is this child a dimwit or just plain cheeky?"

"With your permission, I will speak for the child, as she is very inexperienced," Dete volunteered, after giving Heidi a poke for answering so badly. "She isn't a dimwit nor is she being cheeky.

Indeed, she wouldn't know how. She simply says everything as she sees it. This is the first time she has ever been in a gentleman's house, and she doesn't know any manners. But she is willing and quick to learn, if the lady will make a few allowances for her. She was christened Adelheid, like her mother."

"That name is a lot easier on the tongue," said Miss Rottenmeyer. "But Dete, I have to say she looks a little young. I told you that Miss Clara's companion must be the same age, to share her lessons and other occupations. Clara is over twelve. How old is this child?"

"With your permission, I'm not exactly sure how old she is. She must be only a little younger than that...perhaps ten or so..." Dete began.

"I'm eight. Grandfather told me," Heidi said. Dete gave her another poke, but as Heidi had no idea why, she was undeterred.

"What? Only eight?" cried Miss Rottenmeyer. "That's four years too young. How is that supposed to work? What have you learned, child? What books did you use in your lessons?"

"None," answered Heidi.

"How? What? Then how did you learn to read?" Miss Rottenmeyer continued.

"I haven't learned to read. Nor has Peter," Heidi replied.

"Good gracious! You can't read? You really can't read?" shrieked Miss Rottenmeyer in horror. "Is it possible? Well what on earth have you learned?"

Miss Rottenmeyer heaved herself slowly out of her chair and came closer to examine the new arrival. She didn't look too pleased.

"Nothing," said Heidi with utter honesty.

Miss Rottenmeyer took a minute or two to recover. "Dete," she said, "this is not at all what we discussed. How could you bring this creature here?"

But Dete wasn't to be so easily dissuaded. "If I may, this child is exactly what I thought you described. You said you wanted a child who was different from all other children. So I had to choose this little one, as the older children are all pretty similar where I come from. This child seemed to perfectly fit the description. Anyway I must dash as my mistress is waiting for me, but if she lets me, I'll pop by another time and see how the child is faring." With a quick curtsey, Dete dived out of the door and down the steps.

Miss Rottenmeyer stood there for a moment, thinking of all the reasons the child was unsuitable. Then all at once, she realized she had been left with the girl, and she hurried out of the room after Dete.

Heidi was still standing in the same spot by the door. Until that moment, Clara had watched everything from her wheelchair in silence. Now, however, she waved the little girl over, "Come here," she said.

Heidi came closer to the wheelchair. "Do you prefer Heidi or Adelheid?" Clara asked.

"My name is Heidi, not anything else," was Heidi's answer.

"Then that's what I'll always call you," promised Clara. "I

think it suits you, although I have never heard it before. I've also never seen a girl that looked like you before. Have you always had such wild hair?"

"I think so," replied Heidi.

"Are you happy you came to Frankfurt?" Clara asked.

"No, but tomorrow I'm going home again, and I can bring Grandmother some white bread rolls," Heidi explained.

"You are strange!" exclaimed Clara. "You were brought here to Frankfurt to stay with me and share my lessons, which will be lots of fun, don't you think? You can't read so you are going to learn how, right from the beginning. It was so dreadfully boring before, and the mornings always dragged on forever. You see, every morning at ten, my tutor comes here and my lesson begins. It lasts until two, which is a terribly long time. Sometimes my tutor holds the book so close to his face you'd think he'd become short-sighted, but really he's just yawning behind it. And Miss Rottenmeyer sometimes holds her handkerchief right up to her face, as though she's utterly gripped with something we're reading, but I know full well she's just yawning dreadfully behind it too. All that yawning makes me want to yawn too, but I have to swallow mine, because if I ever let out the teensiest yawn, Miss Rottenmeyer says I must be weakening, and goes to get the cod-liver oil. A dose of cod-liver oil is the absolute worst, so I'd rather just swallow my yawns. But time will go much more quickly now because I can listen to you learning to read."

Heidi shook her head thoughtfully when she heard the part about learning to read.

"Of course you have to learn to read, Heidi. Everybody has to learn to read, and my tutor is very good. He never gets cross and he explains everything. But if he explains something to you and you don't understand it, then just wait and don't say anything, otherwise he'll explain it a lot more and you'll understand it even less. But then later, when you've learned it yourself and know all about it, you'll understand what he meant."

Just then, Miss Rottenmeyer came back into the room. She hadn't caught up with Dete and looked rather annoyed about it. Not only had she been unable to finish telling Dete how unsuitable the child was, she hadn't the faintest idea how she could get rid of Heidi now she was here. She was all the more put out as she felt responsible for the whole mess, having agreed that Heidi should come in the first place.

She rushed agitatedly into the dining room and back, then returned to the dining room to vent her anger at Sebastian, who was gazing at the freshly laid table to check nothing was missing. "You can think your grand thoughts later. Hurry up and make sure the table is ready for supper today rather than tomorrow!"

With this, she bustled past Sebastian and called for Tinette, with such an unpleasant tone that the maid minced in with even tinier steps than usual, and stood there with such a scornful expression on her face. Miss Rottenmeyer didn't dare scold her, but bottled up her anger even more. "Tinette, please prepare the room for our new arrival. Everything is ready. You just need to dust the furniture."

"Hardly worth the effort," Tinette snorted as she flounced out of the room.

In the meantime, Sebastian had rather noisily flung open the double doors into the study. He was furious about Miss Rottenmeyer's comment, but didn't dare argue. He came into the study to push the wheelchair into the dining room. While he stopped to straighten the handle behind the chair, Heidi came right up to him and stared. He growled, "Well? What's so interesting?" which he wouldn't have done had he seen Miss Rottenmeyer in the doorway. She came over just as Heidi answered, "You've got brown eyes just like Goat Peter."

"Is it possible?" Miss Rottenmeyer groaned to herself, clasping her hands together. "Now she's chatting to the servants as though they were friends. The creature hasn't the faintest idea about proper manners."

Sebastian pushed Clara's wheelchair into the dining room, lifted her out of it and sat her at the table. Miss Rottenmeyer sat down next to her and waved Heidi to the place opposite. Nobody else was joining them, and there was plenty of room. The three sat far apart so as to allow Sebastian to come between them with the serving dishes.

A lovely white bread roll lay next to Heidi's plate, and she looked at it with delight. Her feeling of familiarity with Sebastian must have made her trust him, for she sat as still and quiet as a mouse until he approached her to offer her some grilled fish. Then she pointed at the bread roll and asked, "Can I have that?" Sebastian nodded, glancing at Miss Rottenmeyer to see her reaction to the question.

Heidi grabbed the roll and stuffed it quickly into her pocket. Sebastian's face twitched as he tried to stifle his laughter which, of course, was not permitted. He stood next to Heidi silent and unmoving, as he wasn't permitted to speak or to leave until she had helped herself.

Heidi looked at him thoughtfully for a while, then asked, "Am I supposed to eat some of that?" When Sebastian nodded once more, she looked down at her plate and said, "Then give me some." Sebastian struggled to keep his face under control and the dish he was holding began to tremble suspiciously.

"You may place the dish on the table and come back for it later," Miss Rottenmeyer instructed him with a stern face. Sebastian did so and disappeared immediately.

"Adelheid, I see that I must teach you even the basics," Miss Rottenmeyer said with a deep sigh. "Firstly I must teach you how to serve yourself at the table." The lady explained in great detail everything Heidi was supposed to do. "Secondly," she continued, "you must not talk to Sebastian at the table, unless you have a particularly important question or request to make of him. And do not talk to him as though he were part of your family. He is a servant, not your friend, and you should address him as such. Tinette you also address as the maid, politely. Me you must address as the others do, and Clara can decide for herself what you should call her."

"Clara, of course," said Clara.

There followed a long list of rules about getting up and going to bed, coming in and going out of rooms, leaving things tidy and shutting doors, during which Heidi's eyes slowly closed. She had, after all, woken up before five o'clock that morning and come a very long way. She leaned back in her chair and fell fast asleep.

After a long time, Miss Rottenmeyer came to the end of her lecture, and said, "Now think about it, Adelheid. Did you understand it all?"

"Heidi's been asleep for a while," remarked Clara with an amused expression. She couldn't remember when dinner had last been so entertaining.

"The things this child does! It's just not normal!" Miss Rottenmeyer exclaimed in annoyance, and she rang so loudly that Sebastian and Tinette came tripping into the room together. All the noise didn't wake Heidi, however. She could only be roused enough to be led through the study, then through Clara's bedroom and that of Miss Rottenmeyer, to the corner room which had been made up for her.

Chapter Seven

Miss Rottenmeyer has a busy day

When Heidi opened her eyes on her first morning in Frankfurt, she didn't know where she was. She rubbed her eyes hard and looked again, but nothing had changed. She was sitting in a tall, white bed in a huge room with light shining through very long white curtains. There were two armchairs nearby with big flowers all over them. A sofa covered in the same flowers stood against the wall, with a round table in front of it. In the corner was a wash stand with all kinds of things on it Heidi had never seen before.

All of a sudden she realized she was in Frankfurt. The events of the previous day flooded back to her, including the long list of instructions Miss Rottenmeyer had given her. That is, those she'd heard before falling asleep.

Heidi jumped down from her bed and got dressed. Then she rushed to the window to look at the sky and the ground outside. She felt as though she were in a cage behind the long curtains. They were too heavy to push out of the way, so instead she crept beneath them to get to the window.

It was so high that she could only just see out. She didn't find what she was looking for, so she ran to another window, and another, and then back to the first. All the views were the same: walls and windows and more walls. It made Heidi feel anxious.

It was still very early in the morning, as Heidi was used to getting up early on the Alm and running to the door to see what it was like outside – if the sky was blue and the sun was up, if the pine trees were sighing and the little flowers already had their petals open. Just like a newly caged bird trying to find a way out, Heidi flitted from one window to another, to see if she could push them open. But they remained firmly shut, however hard she tried.

"Perhaps I should go outside," she wondered, "and see if I can find the grass and sky." She remembered that yesterday evening she had only seen paving stones outside the house. As she thought about this, there came a knock at the door, and Tinette stuck her head inside and said, "Breakfast is ready."

Heidi didn't understand that this was an invitation to come downstairs. Tinette's scornful expression seemed very clearly to say, "Stay away," rather than "Come with me." So Heidi pulled the little stool from under the table and sat down on it in a corner to wait and see what would happen next.

After a while Miss Rottenmeyer burst through the door. "Whatever is the matter with you Adelheid?" she exclaimed. "Don't you know what 'breakfast' means? Come downstairs now!"

This Heidi understood, and she followed her into the dining room. Clara was already sitting at the table. "Good morning, Heidi," she said smiling. She was looking forward to the day, certain it would prove eventful.

Breakfast passed without incident, with Heidi eating her bread and butter in an acceptable manner. When it was finished, Clara was pushed into the study in her wheelchair, and Miss Rottenmeyer told Heidi to come too, and stay with Clara until the tutor arrived to start their lesson.

"How can you see out of here right down to the ground?" Heidi asked, as soon as they were alone.

"You open a window and look out," said Clara, amused.

"The windows don't open," said Heidi sadly.

"Yes they do," Clara assured her. "You can't open them, and nor can I, but Sebastian will open one if you ask him to."

This was a great relief to Heidi.

Clara started asking about her life at home, and so Heidi told her happily all about the Alm and the goats and the meadows and everything she loved.

Meanwhile the tutor had arrived, but before showing him into the study, Miss Rottenmeyer took him aside for a little chat. She sat down with him in the dining room, and explained the awkward situation she found herself in.

"A little while ago, I wrote to Mr. Sesemann in Paris, where he was staying at the time, to ask whether it would be possible for Clara to have a companion," she began. "Clara had told me she would like someone to keep her company and share her lessons, and I thought it a good idea. After all, it might even allow me the time to get on with more important matters," she added, straightening her spectacles.

"Mr. Sesemann answered that he would gladly grant his daughter's request, with the single condition that any companion living in the house must be treated as his daughter's equal at all times, for he didn't want anyone treated cruelly in his household. Which was a pointless thing to say, as who would want that?

"But I have been dreadfully taken in. The girl who has came does not in the least resemble what I asked for. She is ignorant and uncivilized. And she doesn't even know how to read. Her education would have to start with the alphabet," Miss Rottenmeyer bristled. "Not even there! Her education needs to begin with the very basics of a good upbringing."

She leaned in conspiratorially to the tutor at this point. "I can see only one way out of this terrible situation, and that is if you could explain to Mr. Sesemann that the two girls are at such different levels of ability that they cannot possibly take lessons together without it being detrimental to our dear Clara, who is of course the more able. That will be a good enough reason for Mr. Sesemann to send the girl back to where she came from, and thus release us from this regretful situation." Miss Rottenmeyer leaned back in her chair at this point, looking relieved at the prospect of a solution. "Without your agreement," she told the tutor, "the mistake cannot be corrected, as the gentleman of the house already knows of Heidi's arrival."

However, the tutor was a cautious man, and impartial in his judgements. He offered Miss Rottenmeyer some words of comfort, and assured her that if the new little girl was behind in some areas, she was sure to be ahead in others, so that with some well-planned lessons, the difference could be balanced out.

As soon as Miss Rottenmeyer saw that the tutor wasn't going to back her up, and that he was determined to undertake the teaching of the alphabet, she opened the doors to the study to let him in. She shut them hurriedly behind him and stayed outside, for she detested anything to do with the ABCs.

Striding up and down the dining room, she mulled over the problem of how the serving staff were to address Adelheid. Mr. Sesemann had explicitly said she must be treated the same as his daughter in all respects, which must refer, Miss Rottenmeyer imagined, mainly to the servants.

She didn't have the chance to think anything further about it, as suddenly there was a tremendous crash next door, and a cry for Sebastian's help. She burst into the room. All the exercise books,

textbooks, the inkpot, and a whole heap of school things lay in a heap on the floor with the tablecloth over the top. A black stream of ink flowed from under the tablecloth all the way across the room. Heidi was gone.

"Now we have it!" cried Miss Rottenmeyer, wringing her hands. "Tablecloth, books, everything covered in ink. This has never happened before. It can only be that unhappy creature. There's no doubt about it!"

The tutor was standing in a daze, looking at the scene of destruction before him. Clara however, who was following the unusual happenings and their effects with great enjoyment, explained, "Yes, Heidi did it, but not on purpose. She mustn't be punished as it was only that she was in such a hurry that she took the tablecloth with her and everything else, which landed on the floor. A few stagecoaches drove by at once, which is why she ran out. Perhaps she's never seen a stagecoach before."

"Do you see what I mean now?" Miss Rottenmeyer said to the tutor. "This creature hasn't a clue how to behave properly – no idea what a lesson is, or that during a lesson one must sit still and listen. But where has the little rascal gone? Tell me she hasn't run away. Mr. Sesemann will be..."

Miss Rottenmeyer ran out of the room and down the stairs, where she found Heidi standing in the open front door, looking out. She was gazing up and down the street in consternation.

"What's the matter with you? Why did you run out like that?" Miss Rottenmeyer scolded.

"I heard the wind in the pine trees, but I don't know where they are. I can't hear it any more," Heidi replied, looking disappointedly down the road. The noise, so like that of the wind rushing through the pine trees, had faded with the passing of the coaches.

"Pine trees? Do you think we're in a forest? What ideas you have. Come upstairs and see what you've done." Miss Rottenmeyer climbed the stairs again, and Heidi followed. Upstairs, she stared in wonder at the mess. She hadn't realized she had pulled the tablecloth with her, so eager had she been to rush down and see the pine trees.

"You must never do that again," said Miss Rottenmeyer, pointing at the mess. "In lessons, you sit still on your chair and pay attention. If you cannot stay seated by yourself, then I shall tie you to your chair. Is that understood?"

"Yes," said Heidi. "I can stay seated by myself." She understood now that it was a rule – one must sit still during lessons.

Sebastian and Tinette had to come and clean up the mess. The tutor left, to continue the lesson another time. There had been no time for yawning that day.

Miss Rottenmeyer had already explained to Heidi that Clara had to rest for a while every afternoon, and so Heidi was free to amuse herself during this time. After lunch, Clara went off to lie down and Miss Rottenmeyer retired to her room. Heidi realized this was the time when she was allowed do as she pleased.

She was very glad as she already had an idea about what she wanted to do; it was something that needed help, however. Heidi positioned herself in the middle of the corridor outside the dining room so that the person she needed help from could not pass by unseen.

Indeed, after a short time, Sebastian came up the stairs carrying a big tea tray full of silverware that he was bringing from the kitchen to put away in the dining room cupboard. As he came up the last stair, Heidi went over to him and said very clearly, "Servant-Not-My-Friend."

Sebastian's eyes opened very wide, and he said rather curtly, "What do you mean, Miss?"

"I just want to ask you something," said Heidi. "It's not

something naughty like this morning," she added hesitantly, as she noticed that Sebastian was a little annoyed, and thought it must be to do with the ink on the floor.

"Very well but why did you call me 'Servant-Not-My-Friend'?" Sebastian asked in the same sharp tone.

"That's what I have to call you. Miss Rottenmeyer said so," Heidi confided.

Sebastian laughed so loudly that Heidi stared at him. She saw nothing funny in what she'd said. But Sebastian understood perfectly what Miss Rottenmeyer must have told the little girl, and said warmly, "That's alright then, Little Miss. Do go on."

"I'm not called Little Miss. I'm called Heidi," she replied, somewhat annoyed herself.

"I know. But Miss Rottenmeyer has told me to call you Miss," said Sebastian.

"Has she? Then that's what I must be called," Heidi conceded. She understood full well that Miss Rottenmeyer's word was the law in this household. She sighed, however, and said, "Now I've got three names."

"What was it that Miss wanted to ask me?" Sebastian asked, going into the dining room with his silverware.

"How do you open a window, Sebastian?"

"Just like this," Sebastian answered, flinging open the huge window.

Heidi ran over to it, but she was too small to see out properly.

Sebastian picked up a chair and set it down by the window, "Here, this is so you can see out."

Delighted, Heidi clambered up onto the chair. At last she could see out of the window! But the view so disappointed her that she soon drew her head back in. "You can only see the paved street, nothing else," Heidi said sadly. "What do you see if you look out from the other side of the house, Sebastian?"

"The same," he answered.

"But where can you go to see far, far across the whole valley?"

"You'd have to go to the top of a big tower, a church tower, like that one over there with the gold bell on top. From way up there you can see everything."

Heidi got down from the chair hurriedly, ran to the door, down the stairs and out onto the street. But it wasn't how she'd imagined. From upstairs, she could see the church tower with the golden bell, and it had looked as if she only needed to cross the street to reach it. But Heidi went all down the street and didn't reach it. She ran down one street and another, and another, and still couldn't see the tower. Lots of people went by but they were all in such a rush, Heidi didn't think they would have time to help her. Then she saw a young boy standing on a street corner with a barrel organ on his back and a very strange looking animal on his arm. Heidi ran over to him and said, "Where is the tower with the gold bell on top?"

"Don't know," was the answer.

"Who would know where it is?" asked Heidi.

"Don't know."

"Do you know a church with a big tower?"

"Of course."

"Take me there!"

"Show me what you'll give me if I do."

Heidi rummaged in her pockets. She brought out a little picture of a pretty wreath of roses. She looked at it for a while, regretfully. Clara had only given it to her only that morning, and she didn't want to part with it. But to see the valley and far over the cliffs... "Here," she said holding the picture out. "Do you want this?"

The boy shook his head.

Heidi slipped the postcard back into her pocket feeling relieved. "What then?" she asked.

"Money."

"I don't have any, but Clara does. She'll give me some for you. How much do you want?"

"Twenty pennies."

"Alright. Let's go."

The two children went off down the street. On the way, Heidi asked her guide what the thing was on his back, and he explained that it was an organ, which made wonderful music when he turned the handle. They came to an old church with a tall tower, and the boy stopped and said, "There it is."

"How do I get in?" asked Heidi.

"Don't know," came the reply.

"Do you think I can ring, like you're supposed to for Sebastian?"

"Don't know."

Heidi discovered a bell on the wall and pulled it with all her might. "When I go up, you have to wait for me here to show me the way back again. I won't find it by myself."

"What'll you give me?"

"What do I have to give you this time?"

"Another twenty pennies."

The door creaked open and an old man peered out, first curiously, then angrily, at the two children. "What are you doing, ringing for me. Can't you read? It says only those who want to climb the tower should ring."

The boy pointed silently at Heidi, who said, "I want to climb the tower."

"What for? Did someone send you?" said the towerkeeper.

"No. I want to go up so I can look down," Heidi replied.

"Get away from here, both of you, and don't try this funny business again, or you'll be in trouble." The old man turned away and was going to shut the door, but Heidi tugged his robe and begged, "Just once."

He looked around and was so moved by the beseeching look in Heidi's eyes, that he said gruffly, "Oh, come on then, if it means that much to you."

The boy sat down on the stone step in front of the door, showing quite clearly that he didn't want to come. So the towerkeeper took Heidi's hand and together they climbed the many, many steps inside. The steps grew narrower and narrower, and seemed to go on forever until, after the last few tiny steps, they were at the top. The towerkeeper lifted Heidi up and held her at the open window. "There you go, look down," he said.

Heidi looked down at the sea of roofs, towers and chimneys. Disappointed, she pulled back her head. "It's not what I thought," she said.

"See? What does a little child know about a good view? Come down now and don't ring my bell again." The towerkeeper put Heidi back down and went ahead of her down the narrow steps. Where they grew wider, there was a door on the left into the towerkeeper's little room. Next to it, where the roof sloped down to the floor, sat a large tabby cat in front of a basket. It growled, because its kittens were in the basket and it wanted to warn the passers-by not to meddle with them.

Heidi stopped and stared at it. She'd never seen such a big cat before. Lots of mice lived in the old tower, and this cat easily caught a dozen or so for dinner every day. The towerkeeper saw how taken Heidi was with it and said, "She won't harm you if I'm with you. Come and see her kittens."

Heidi went with him to the basket and cried, "Oh, the sweet little things!" She dived around the basket looking at all the kittens, and admiring them as they clambered over one another and played and leaped and wrestled in the basket.

The towerkeeper smiled at Heidi's delight, and said, "Would you like one?"

"To keep? For myself?" gasped Heidi, scarcely able to believe her luck.

"Certainly. You can take them all if you have space," said the old man, who was glad of the chance to get rid of them so easily.

Heidi was beside herself with happiness. The kittens would have so much space in the big house, and how surprised and pleased Clara would be with the dear little things!

"But how can I carry them all?" Heidi asked, trying to catch one in her hands. She jumped back in shock as the mother cat leaped at her, growling furiously.

"I can bring them. Just tell me where," said the towerkeeper, stroking his cat to calm her down. She was after all his dear old friend and had lived with him in the tower for many years.

"To Mr. Sesemann's house. It's the one with the big, gold dog head on the door, with a ring in its mouth," Heidi explained.

The old man had been the keeper of the tower for many, long years and knew every house around it. Besides that, Sebastian was a good friend of his, so he knew very well where Heidi meant. "Who shall I say they are for? You aren't part of Mr. Sesemann's family, are you?"

"No. Say they are for Clara. She'll be so pleased to be given all these kittens!"

The towerkeeper started to go downstairs, but Heidi couldn't tear herself away from the basket. "If only I could take two now, one for me and one for Clara... May I?"

"Alright. Wait a minute," said the old man. Carefully, he carried the cat into his little room and gave her a dish of food to eat. Then he shut the door on her and said, "Now you can take two."

Heidi picked a white one and a yellow-and-white striped one, and put one in her right pocket and one in her left.

They went down the stairs to find the boy waiting on the doorstep. After the towerkeeper had shut the door, Heidi asked him, "Which way do we go to get to Mr. Sesemann's house?"

"Don't know," came the reply.

Heidi started to describe the house as far as she could remember it, the door, the windows and the front steps, but the boy shook his head. He didn't know the house.

"From one of the windows you can see a roof that goes like this," Heidi said, drawing a big zigzag in the air with her finger.

At that the boy jumped up. That was a landmark he knew. He wove his way through the streets with Heidi following behind, and in a short while they were standing by Mr. Sesemann's front door.

Heidi pulled the bell and Sebastian appeared. As soon as he saw Heidi, he said, "Quick! Quick!" Heidi hurried inside and he shut the door. The boy was left outside, baffled and unnoticed.

"Quick, Miss," Sebastian urged again. "Go straight into the dining room and sit down. Miss Rottenmeyer looks like a loaded cannon. Whatever possessed you to run off like that?"

Heidi went in. Miss Rottenmeyer did not look up. Clara didn't say anything either and it was strangely quiet. Heidi sat down and Sebastian pushed her chair in for her. Then Miss Rottenmeyer began, in the gravest tone, "Adelheid, I will speak to you later. For now I will just say this: you have behaved dreadfully and must be punished. You left the house without asking, without anyone knowing a thing about it, and have been cavorting around goodness knows where until evening. It is completely unacceptable."

"Meow," came a reply.

The lady's fury mounted. "Do you think, Adelheid," she said raising her voice, "that after all the trouble you've caused it's a good idea to make some silly joke? You had better watch out, young lady!"

"But it's not—" Heidi began.

"Meow, meow!"

It was all Sebastian could do to stop himself from laughing. He practically threw the serving dish onto the table and dived out of the room.

"That's quite enough," Miss Rottenmeyer tried to shout, her voice hoarse with fury. "Get up at once and leave the room."

Heidi stood up in alarm. "But it's not—"

"Meow, meow!"

"Heidi," Clara said, "why do you keep saying 'Meow' when you can see how angry it's making Miss Rottenmeyer?"

"But it's not me, it's the kittens," Heidi finally managed to say.

"What? How? Kittens?" shrieked Miss Rottenmeyer. "Sebastian! Tinette! Search for the horrid things! Catch them immediately!" With that, she fled into the study and slammed the double doors closed. Miss Rottenmeyer hated kittens more than anything else on earth.

Outside the dining room, Sebastian had to wait until he'd finished laughing before he could come back in. He had seen a little kitten poking out of Heidi's pocket as he had served her and knew that there was going to be an uproar. He'd only just managed to control himself enough to put down the dish before leaving the room. When he had finally stopped laughing, he went back into the dining room, some time after the cries for help had been uttered.

There he found a calm and happy scene. Clara had the kittens on her lap and Heidi was kneeling beside her. They were both playing delightedly with the dainty little animals.

"Sebastian, you must help us," Clara said pleadingly. "You have to find a hiding place for the kittens, where Miss Rottenmeyer won't find them. She's scared of them, and wants them gone. But we want to keep the sweet little things, and play with them whenever we're alone. Where could we hide them?"

"I'll take care of it, Miss Clara," Sebastian said willingly. "I'll make up a nice little bed in a basket and put them somewhere the ferocious lady doesn't ever go. You can count on me." Sebastian started to go about his business, chuckling to himself as he thought, "What a commotion." He was rather enjoying seeing Miss Rottenmeyer stirred up.

Only after a long time, when bedtime was approaching, did Miss Rottenmeyer dare open the door a tiny crack and call, "Have you disposed of those nasty creatures?"

"Yes, yes," replied Sebastian, who had found things to keep himself busy in the dining room in anticipation of this question. He quickly scooped the two kittens off Clara's lap and disappeared with them.

The particular talking-to that Miss Rottenmeyer had in mind for Heidi was postponed until the following day. Miss Rottenmeyer was far too exhausted from all the feelings of irritation and fury and terror that Heidi had unwittingly caused in her. She went to bed without another word. Clara and Heidi followed, happy in the knowledge that their kittens would have a safe, snug bed of their own.

Chapter Eight

A commotion at Mr. Sesemann's

Shortly after Sebastian had shown the tutor into the study the following morning, the doorbell rang for a second time. It was so loud that Sebastian shot down the stairs thinking, "Only Mr. Sesemann rings like that. He must have come home unexpectedly." He flung open the door to find a ragged boy with a barrel organ on his back standing on the doorstep. "What's all this?" Sebastian barked. "I'll teach you, pulling bells like that. What are you doing here?"

"I have to see Clara," the boy replied.

"You dirty little street urchin. Why can't you call her 'Miss Clara' like the rest of us? What business have you calling on Miss Clara anyway?" Sebastian snapped.

"She owes me forty pennies," said the boy.

"You're not right in the head! How do you even know that Miss Clara lives here?"

"I showed her the way yesterday – that's twenty – and the way back – that's forty!"

"You're talking nonsense. Miss Clara doesn't ever go out because she can't walk. Get back to where you came from before I help you there."

But the boy wouldn't be frightened off. He stayed right where he was and said drily, "I saw her yesterday in the street and I can describe her: she has wild hair and dark eyes and she doesn't talk like us."

"Aha," thought Sebastian, chuckling inwardly. "That's the Little Miss. She's been up to more mischief." Then he pulled the boy inside and said, "Very well, follow me. Wait outside this door until I come out again. When I let you in, you can start playing some music right away. The young lady will like that."

Upstairs, he knocked on the door of the study and was called inside. "There's a little boy here, who has asked to see Miss Clara."

Clara was delighted at the unusual turn of events. "Let him in right away," she said.

The boy came in and began to play his barrel organ as directed. Miss Rottenmeyer, who had busied herself in the dining room so as to avoid the ABCs, pricked up her ears. Was the music coming from the street below? It sounded so close. How could barrel-organ music be coming from the study? But it really seemed to be. She rushed through the dining room and flung open the door. There – to her disbelief – stood a ragged organ player in the middle of the study, industriously turning the handle of his instrument. The tutor appeared to be trying to say something, but could not be heard. Clara and Heidi were listening to the music with expressions of delight on their faces.

"Stop immediately!" Miss Rottenmeyer shouted. Her voice was drowned out by the music. She ran towards the boy, but suddenly felt something creep between her feet. She looked down to see a horrid, dark creature on the floor. It was a tortoise! Miss Rottenmeyer jumped higher into the air than she had in years and screamed for all she was worth, "Sebastian! Sebastian!"

Suddenly the organ player stopped playing, as this time the voice had drowned out the music. Sebastian stood outside the half-open door doubled over with laughter, for he had been watching everything. Eventually he came in. Miss Rottenmeyer had sunk into a chair, and said, "Take them away – boy and beast. Take them away, Sebastian. Right now!"

Sebastian obeyed willingly. He pulled the boy, who quickly picked up his tortoise, out of the room. Outside he pressed some coins into his hand, saying, "Forty from Miss Clara and another forty for the music. You did well." Then he showed him out of the house.

In the study everything had settled down again. The lesson continued with Miss Rottenmeyer sitting in the room to ward off any more terrible goings-on. She intended to wait until after the lesson to investigate the incident and punish those responsible.

There came another knock at the door. This time Sebastian came in with the news that a large basket had been delivered that was to be given to Miss Clara right away.

"To me?" asked Clara astonished, burning with curiosity at what it could possibly be. "Show it to me please. Let me see what it looks like." Sebastian brought the covered basket in and hastened out of the room.

"I think you should finish your lessons before opening the basket," Miss Rottenmeyer remarked.

Clara couldn't imagine what anyone could have sent her. She looked longingly at the basket. In the middle of reciting something, she suddenly broke off and said to the tutor, "Sir, couldn't I just peek inside quickly, so I know what it is, and then carry on?"

"Well, one could argue either way," replied the tutor. "In the argument *for*, one could say that if your full attention can be given to the lesson..." He didn't have a chance to finish. The lid of the basket was loose and, all at once, kittens began to clamber out – one, two, three, more – so unbelievably quickly, that all of a sudden the room was full of them. They leaped over the tutor's boots, chewed on his laces, climbed up Miss Rottenmeyer's skirt, clawed around her feet, jumped onto Clara's chair, scratching, scrabbling and meowing. It was total chaos.

Clara called out delightedly again and again, "Oh, the sweet little things! They're so funny, the way they leap about. Look, look, Heidi. Here! There! This one! Look at that one!"

Heidi happily leaped all around the room after them. The tutor stood distractedly at the table, waving first one foot in the air and then the other in an attempt to escape the scratching and scrabbling.

At first, Miss Rottenmeyer sat in her chair, speechless with horror. Then she began to scream with all her might, "Tinette! Tinette! Sebastian! Sebastian!" She didn't dare get to her feet in case all the little monsters turned on her.

Eventually, after repeated cries for help, Sebastian and Tinette came in. They packed the kittens one after the other into the basket and took it away to the secret hiding place that had been made up for the other two kittens the day before.

There had been no time for yawning in today's lesson either. Late that evening, when Miss Rottenmeyer had recovered from all the excitement, she summoned Sebastian and Tinette to the study for a thorough investigation of the reprehensible events of the day. It was then that it came out, how Heidi had been responsible for it all. Miss Rottenmeyer sat there, white with rage, and unable to speak a word about the discovery. She dismissed Sebastian and Tinette with a wave of her hand. Then she turned to Heidi, who was standing next to Clara's wheelchair, and didn't really understand what she'd done wrong.

"Adelheid," she began in a severe tone, "I only know of one punishment that could possibly suit you, for you are a complete barbarian. We shall see if locking you in a dark cellar with the black beetles and rats will teach you a lesson, so you don't think of doing anything like this again."

Heidi listened to her punishment quietly and with amazement. She had never been in a cellar like that. The room in the Alm hut that Grandfather called a cellar was the place he stored the finished cheeses and the fresh milk, and it was a very comforting, inviting place to be. She'd never seen a black beetle or a rat.

But Clara cried out piteously, "No, no, Miss Rottenmeyer. You have to wait until Papa is here. He wrote saying he's coming soon. I'll tell him everything and he will say what should be done with Heidi."

Miss Rottenmeyer was overruled and couldn't do anything about it, particularly as Mr. Sesemann really was expected to arrive soon. She stood up and said grimly, "Very well, Clara, but I will have words with Mr. Sesemann myself about this." Then she left the room.

A couple of undisturbed days went by, but Miss Rottenmeyer did not calm down. The thought that she had been utterly deceived from the beginning about Heidi's character tormented her hourly. It seemed to her that since the girl's arrival everything in the Sesemann household had become disjointed and would never be the same again.

Clara on the other hand was very happy. She was no longer bored, as Heidi helped the time go by very quickly in their lessons. She got the letters of the alphabet confused all the time, and simply couldn't learn them. Whenever the tutor tried to help by describing their shape, mentioning horns or a snout, she would burst out joyfully, "It's a goat!" or "It's an eagle!" His descriptions gave rise to all kinds of images in her mind, but no letters.

In the late afternoons, Heidi would sit with Clara and tell her all about the Alm and her life there. She talked about it so often and at such length, that the longing in her would grow and grow, and she always concluded, "I really must go home. Tomorrow I will go, for sure." But Clara would calm her down and say she needed to wait until Papa came at least, and then they would see what to do next.

Heidi always agreed, comforting herself with the secret knowledge that with every day she stayed, the heap of white bread rolls she was saving for Grandmother grew by two. Every morning and evening at the dinner table, she would pocket the roll by her plate. She couldn't possibly eat the rolls herself, while Grandmother only had hard, black bread.

Every afternoon after lunch, Heidi sat alone in her room for a couple of hours. She had gathered that she wasn't allowed to roam around freely in Frankfurt the way she had on the Alm, so she didn't try to any more. She wasn't allowed to talk to Sebastian in the dining room, as Miss Rottenmeyer had forbidden that too, and it didn't occur to her to try to talk to Tinette. Heidi always shied away from meeting the maid, who only ever spoke to her in a sneering tone or to make fun of her. Heidi quickly realized that this was how she was with everything and everyone.

So Heidi sat in her room every day with little to do except imagine how green the Alm would be again and how the little, yellow flowers would be glittering in the sunshine and everything all around would be lit up by the sun – the snow and the mountains and the whole, wide valley. She longed to be there so much that sometimes she could hardly bear it.

She remembered her aunt saying that she would be able to go home if she wanted to. So one day, when Heidi could stand it no longer, she stuffed all the bread rolls she'd saved into her large red shawl, put on her straw hat, and set off.

She'd gone no further than the front door when she stumbled across an obstacle in the shape of Miss Rottenmeyer, who was just coming in. The lady stood and looked Heidi up and down in great astonishment, her gaze lingering on the stuffed red shawl. Then she burst out, "What's all this? Have I not expressly forbidden you to go sneaking around? Now you're doing so again and, what's more, you're dressed like a vagabond!"

"I'm not sneaking around. I'm just going home," Heidi replied in fright.

"How? What? You want to go home, do you?" Miss Rottenmeyer clapped her hands together in outrage. "Running away! If Mr. Sesemann hears of this – running away from his house. And what is it that doesn't suit you? Have you not been treated better than you deserve to be? Is something lacking? Have you ever in your life been fed and served in the way you have here? Answer me!"

"No," said Heidi.

"I knew it!" said the lady with feeling. "There is nothing lacking, absolutely nothing. You are an unbelievably ungrateful thing. You don't know how lucky you are!"

But then everything that Heidi had been feeling came spilling out. "I just want to go home. If I stay away too long Snowflake will cry, and Grandmother is expecting me, and Goldfinch will be beaten if Goat Peter doesn't get his cheese, and here you can never see how the sun says good night to the mountains, and if the eagle flew over Frankfurt, he would cry much more loudly to see so many people crammed together making each other cross instead of going up onto the cliffs where you feel so much better."

"Good gracious, the child's lost her mind," cried Miss Rottenmeyer. She rushed up the stairs in fright and crashed right into Sebastian who was on his way down. "Get that unfortunate creature back upstairs right away," she ordered, rubbing her head. She had bumped it rather hard against Sebastian's.

"Yes, very well, thank you, right away," replied Sebastian, rubbing his own. He'd bumped his head even harder.

Heidi stood rooted to the spot. Her eyes burned and her whole body trembled with emotion. "Up to mischief again?" Sebastian asked her in a jolly voice. But Heidi didn't move a muscle. Sebastian looked at her more closely, then patted her amiably on the shoulder and said, "Now, now, Little Miss mustn't take it to heart. Chin up, that's the main thing! She just knocked a hole in my head, but we mustn't let it get us down. Still not budging? We have to go up, she's ordered it."

Heidi went up the stairs, but slowly and quietly and not at all in her usual manner. Sebastian was very sorry to see this. He followed behind, saying encouraging things to her: "Don't give up. Don't be sad. Keep going. We've got such a good Little Miss here, who hasn't cried the whole time she's been with us. Other little girls of her age cry twelve times a day – everybody knows that. The kittens are having fun upstairs – they're leaping around like fools in their hiding place. We'll go and see them afterwards, when the lady's not there, alright?"

Heidi nodded her head a little, but so joylessly, that it cut Sebastian to the quick. He could only watch sympathetically as she slipped away to her room.

At supper, Miss Rottenmeyer didn't say a word, but was strangely watchful, constantly glancing at Heidi as though she expected her to do something outrageous at any moment. Heidi sat at the table as quiet as a mouse. She didn't move, nor did she eat or drink anything. She just quickly tucked the bread roll into her pocket as usual.

The following morning, when the tutor came up the stairs, Miss Rottenmeyer beckoned him secretively into the dining room and shared her concern: that the change of scene, the unaccustomed way of life, all the unfamiliar surroundings had driven the girl out of her mind. She told him about Heidi's attempt to run away and repeated all she could remember of the strange things the little girl had said.

"On the one hand I've observed Adelheid to be somewhat eccentric," replied the tutor, "but on the other she is certainly sane. I believe with the correct handling, I can achieve the balance that I have in mind," he assured her. "I think it is more relevant to note that I have so far been unable teach her the alphabet. She is incapable, for one reason or another, of learning her letters."

Miss Rottenmeyer felt much calmer and let the tutor go about his work. Late that afternoon she remembered Heidi's outfit during her attempted escape, and decided that the child should be properly clothed in some of Clara's cast-offs before Mr. Sesemann returned. She shared the idea with Clara, who was very enthusiasic about it and wanted to give Heidi a whole load of clothes, handkerchiefs and hats.

Miss Rottenmeyer went to Heidi's room to look through her wardrobe and sort out what could be kept and what ought to be thrown out. But in a couple of minutes she returned with a look of disgust on her face. "What do you think I found, Adelheid?" she cried. "In the wardrobe, where only clothes are meant to be kept, Adelheid, what do I find? A heap of bread rolls! Bread rolls, Clara, in the wardrobe! She's collected a whole heap of them! – Tinette!" she called. "Take the old bread rolls out of Adelheid's cupboard and the squashed straw hat from her table and throw them away."

"No! No!" Heidi wailed. "I have to have the hat and the bread rolls are for Grandmother." She tried to run after Tinette but Miss Rottenmeyer seized her.

"You will stay here and that rubbish will be thrown away as is right and proper," she said firmly, holding the child back.

Heidi flung herself down on Clara's chair and burst into tears. Her crying grew louder and louder and more and more disconsolate. Between sobs she gulped, "Now Grandmother won't have any bread rolls. They were for Grandmother and now they're all gone and she won't have any!" Heidi wept as though her heart would break.

Miss Rottenmeyer ran out of the room. But Clara felt terribly sorry for Heidi. "Please don't cry," she begged her. "Listen, I promise that when you go home, I'll give you just as many bread rolls for Grandmother as you had and more. They'll be fresh and soft, not like those old ones which must have been stale by now. Come on Heidi, please stop crying."

Heidi couldn't stop sobbing for a while, but she understood what Clara was saying, and clung to it. Otherwise she wouldn't have been able to stop at all. She had to make sure of the promise and, between her last fits of sobbing, kept asking Clara, "You promise you'll give me as many as I had for Grandmother?"

"I promise I will, and more besides. So cheer up now."

That evening Heidi still had red eyes from weeping when she came down for supper. When she saw the bread roll by her plate she couldn't help but let out another sob. But she forced herself to stop, for she knew that one must be quiet at the dinner table.

Whenever Sebastian came anywhere near Heidi he kept on making the strangest faces. He pointed to his head, then Heidi's, then nodded and scrunched up his eyes, as if to say, "Don't worry. I've taken care of it for you."

When Heidi went to her room to go to bed later on, she found her squashed straw hat hidden under the covers. Delighted, she pulled it out and hugged it for pure joy, squashing it even more. Then she hid it, wrapped tightly in a handkerchief, in the furthest corner of her cupboard.

That was what Sebastian had been trying to tell her during supper. He'd been in the dining room when Tinette had been summoned, and followed her to Heidi's room. When Tinette came out with the heap of bread and a hat on top, he'd swept the hat off the pile, saying, "I'll deal with this," and so had been able to save the hat for Heidi.

Chapter Nine

Mr. Sesemann hears all sorts of news

A few days later, the Sesemann house was a hive of activity. The man of the house had just returned from his travels, and Tinette and Sebastian were busy running up and down the stairs, carrying load after load from his carriage. He always brought lots of lovely things with him when he came home.

Mr. Sesemann first went to his daughter's room to say hello. Heidi was sitting with her, as it was late afternoon and the two girls were always together at that time.

Clara greeted her father tenderly, for she adored him. He was a loving father, and greeted his dear little Clara with just as much tenderness. Then he held out his hand to Heidi, who had retreated quietly into the corner, and said amiably, "And this is our little

Swiss girl. Come and shake hands with me. That's right. Now tell me, are you and Clara good friends? No bickering and getting cross and crying and then making up again all the time?"

"No, Clara is always nice to me," answered Heidi.

"And Heidi never bickers either, Papa," Clara added quickly.

"That's good. That's what I like to hear," Mr. Sesemann said, standing up. "Now you must let me go and have lunch, as I haven't eaten yet. But afterwards I'll come back and show you what I've brought home."

Mr. Sesemann went into the dining room, where Miss Rottenmeyer was looking over the table that had been laid for his lunch. When Mr. Sesemann sat down, Miss Rottenmeyer took her place opposite him looking like the very embodiment of bad news. "What is it, Miss Rottenmeyer?" asked Mr. Sesemann. "You are sitting there with the most terrifying face. Whatever is the matter? Little Clara seems quite cheerful."

"Mr. Sesemann," the lady began gravely, "this affects Clara too. We have been most dreadfully deceived."

"How?" said Mr. Sesemann, taking a leisurely sip of wine.

"We decided, as you know, Mr. Sesemann, to take in a playmate for Clara. And as I know that you only want the best for your daughter, I had the idea of getting a Swiss girl, for I hoped to have one of those wonderful children I'd read about in books. Those who are brought up in the pure mountain air, and move through life without touching the ground, one might say."

"I believe that even Swiss children have to touch the ground to get anywhere," remarked Mr. Sesemann. "Otherwise they would be born with wings rather than feet."

"Oh, you know what I mean, Mr. Sesemann," Miss Rottenmeyer said. "I mean one of those beings from the pure mountain regions that waft around like ideal spirits."

"And what would my Clara do with an ideal spirit such as you describe, Miss Rottenmeyer?"

"I'm not joking, Mr. Sesemann. This matter is more serious than you think. I have been dreadfully deceived."

"What is it that's so awful? I see nothing dreadful about the child at all," Mr. Sesemann said calmly.

"Let me tell you, Mr. Sesemann, that this creature has filled your house with all manner of people and animals in your absence. You can ask the tutor all about it."

"Animals? What am I to make of that, Miss Rottenmeyer?"

"What is anyone to make of it, indeed! The creature is impossible to understand. It's my belief she has a seriously disturbed mind."

Until this point, Mr. Sesemann hadn't taken the matter at all seriously, but a disturbed mind? Something like that could affect his daughter. He examined Miss Rottenmeyer's face, to try to work out whether it was in fact her mind which was disturbed. At that moment, the door opened and the tutor was announced.

"Aha, the tutor can perhaps help us with the answer. Come in, my dear sir," called Mr. Sesemann. "Come and have a cup of coffee with me. Sit down, do. Now tell me, what's all this about my daughter's playmate bringing animals into the house? And what is the state of her mind?"

The tutor had first to express his joy at Mr. Sesemann's safe return and to welcome him back, which was the reason he had come. When Mr. Sesemann pressed him to answer the points he had raised, the tutor began: "If I am to say something about this young lady's conduct, Mr. Sesemann, then I should first like to point out that if on the one hand there is a lack of development, which is the result, more or less, of a careless upbringing, or perhaps more accurately, a delayed education, and due more or less to upbringing on a mountain, which if it were not too lengthy could have a positive..."

"My dear sir," Mr. Sesemann interrupted. "You're causing yourself too much bother. Just tell me, did the child give you a shock by bringing in any animals, and what do you think of the effects on my little daughter?"

"I don't want to criticize the young lady too harshly," the tutor began again, "for even if on the one hand she lacks social experience, due to her more or less uncultivated life before she moved to Frankfurt, which would account wholly or partially for the lack of development, on the other hand she may be endowed with certain positive qualities..."

"Please excuse me," said Mr. Sesemann. "No, don't get up. I –

I just have to go and see my daughter." He fled from the dining room and didn't come back.

Over in the study, he sat down by his little daughter. Heidi had stood up and Mr. Sesemann turned to her and said, "Listen, little one, please could you go and fetch me – just a minute – fetch me –" Mr. Sesemann couldn't think what he could need, but really wanted to send Heidi away for a moment. "Please fetch me a glass of water."

"Fresh water?" Heidi asked.

"Yes, yes, nice fresh water!" replied Mr. Sesemann. Heidi disappeared. "Now, my dear little Clara," her Papa said, pushing his chair closer to his daughter and taking her hand in his, "tell me something – as clearly and concisely as you can – what animals has your playmate brought into the house? And why does Miss Rottenmeyer think she is not quite right in the head? Can you explain it all to me?"

Clara could indeed. Miss Rottenmeyer had told her the confusing things Heidi had said, all of which made perfect sense to Clara. First she told her father all about the tortoise and the kittens, then she explained Heidi's strange outburst which had unnerved Miss Rottenmeyer so much. Mr. Sesemann laughed heartily at it all. "So you're not tired of the girl, Clara? You don't want me to send her home?" he asked.

"No, no, Papa. Don't do that!" Clara cried out defensively. "Since Heidi arrived, something exciting happens every single day,

and time flies by, unlike it used to, when nothing ever happened. And Heidi talks to me so much about everything."

"Very well, very well, Clara. Here's your friend coming back again. Did you fetch me some nice fresh water, then?"

"Yes, fresh from the fountain," Heidi replied.

"You didn't walk all the way to the fountain yourself, did you, Heidi?" asked Clara.

"Of course, to get really fresh water. But I had to go quite far because there was a crowd at the first fountain. So I went up the street, but there were just as many people at the second fountain. So I went to another street and got the water there, and a gentleman with white hair said to say hello to Mr. Sesemann."

"The expedition was a success," Mr. Sesemann laughed. "Who was the gentleman?"

"He came past the fountain and stopped and asked, 'Who are you fetching water for?' And when I said, 'Mr. Sesemann', he laughed a lot and said to say hello to Mr. Sesemann and he hoped you enjoyed the water."

"Oh yes? Can you describe him a bit more?"

"He had a friendly laugh and a thick, gold chain which had a gold thing hanging from it with a red stone, and he has a cane with a horse's head on top."

"That's the doctor!" "That's my old friend the doctor," cried Clara and Mr. Sesemann in unison, and Mr. Sesemann chuckled at the thought of his old friend and what he must have thought of his new method of getting a drink of water.

The same evening, Mr. Sesemann sat down in the dining room with Miss Rottenmeyer in order to discuss household matters. He explained to her that his daughter's playmate would be staying. He found her to be in her right mind, and his daughter enjoyed her company more than anyone else's. He added very firmly, "Furthermore, I don't want you to criticize her odd little ways. But you're not to worry, Miss Rottenmeyer. You don't have to deal with the child alone, as someone will soon be here who can help. My mother is coming to stay for a nice long time, and she knows how to deal with anyone, doesn't she, Miss Rottenmeyer?"

"Oh yes, that's certainly true, Mr. Sesemann," replied the lady, although she didn't look particularly relieved by the offer of help.

Mr. Sesemann was only home for a short break this time. After two weeks, his business called him away once more to Paris. His daughter was upset he was leaving, but he consoled her with the news that her Grandmamma would be arriving shortly.

Mr. Sesemann had only just left, when a letter came announcing Mrs. Sesemann's departure from Holstein where she lived, and her arrival the very next day. She requested that a coach and horses be sent to the station to pick her up.

Clara was overjoyed at the news and told Heidi so much about Grandmamma, that Heidi also began to call her 'Grandmamma', which caused Miss Rottenmeyer to look at her disapprovingly. Heidi scarcely noticed, as Miss Rottenmeyer was always looking at her disapprovingly.

However, as they said good night later that evening, Miss Rottenmeyer called Heidi first into her room in order to tell her never to call the lady 'Grandmamma' but to use the title 'Madam'. When Heidi gave her a doubtful look, Miss Rottenmeyer said, "Do you understand?" She gave such a glare as she said it that Heidi didn't dare ask for an explanation, even though she actually hadn't understood at all.

Chapter Ten

Grandmamma

The following evening, the Sesemann house was full of anticipation. From all the efforts being made, it was clear that the lady arriving was respected by everyone, and her opinion was held in high esteem. Tinette had put on a brand new white cap. Sebastian had collected a whole load of footstools, and put them in every possible place the lady could choose to sit, so she would have somewhere to rest her feet. Miss Rottenmeyer went about the house overseeing everything with a very upright posture, as if to show that although someone of great note was about to arrive, her own importance was not about to be extinguished.

The carriage drew up to the front door and Sebastian and Tinette rushed downstairs. Miss Rottenmeyer, whose duty it was to be there to welcome Mrs. Sesemann, followed slowly, looking stately. She had ordered Heidi to stay in her room and wait there until she was summoned, as Grandmamma would first want to see Clara on her own.

Heidi sat in the corner of her room and pondered what she was to call Grandmamma. It wasn't long before Tinette stuck her head around the door. "Go to the study," she said, in her usual curt tone.

Heidi hadn't dared ask Miss Rottenmeyer what she had meant by her little chat, but she thought she'd probably just made a mistake, as one always said 'Mr.' or 'Mrs.' in front of a name. When she opened the door to the study, Grandmamma said in a very friendly way, "Here she comes! Come here and let me look at you, my dear."

So Heidi came in and said in her clear voice, "Good afternoon, Mrs. Madam."

"Well, well," said Grandmamma, laughing. "Is that what they call people where you come from? Is it usual in the Alps?"

"No, I've never heard anyone called that before," Heidi replied.

"Nor have I," Grandmamma laughed again, and patted Heidi's cheek amiably. "Children always just call me Grandmamma. Do you think you can do that?"

"Oh yes," Heidi assured her. "That's what I'm used to saying."

"Ah, now I understand," said Grandmamma and nodded with amusement. She looked at Heidi properly for a few moments.

Heidi looked earnestly back into her eyes because the look that shone from them was so warm-hearted it made her feel good. Heidi liked Grandmamma so much that she wanted to look and look at her. She had such lovely white hair, and a pretty lace cap on her head with two wide ribbons hanging down which fluttered about all the time, as if there were a constant breeze around her. It made Grandmamma seem very special to Heidi.

"What's your name, child?" asked Grandmamma.

"I'm called Heidi. But now I'm supposed to answer to Adelheid..." Heidi stopped short, feeling a little guilty as she remembered that she still forgot to answer when Miss Rottenmeyer called, "Adelheid!" And, moreover, Miss Rottenmeyer had just come into the room.

"Mrs. Sesemann will no doubt understand," Miss Rottenmeyer said, "I had to choose a name that people could say without feeling awkward, if only for the servants' sake."

"My dear Rottenmeyer," countered Mrs. Sesemann, "if a person is called 'Heidi' and is used to that name, then I will call her 'Heidi', and that's that."

Miss Rottenmeyer didn't like the old lady calling her by her surname, but she couldn't do anything about it: Grandmamma had her own ways of doing things, and nothing would change them. As for Grandmamma, she was a sharp old lady, with all her wits about her, and had seen what was going on in the house the moment she came through the door.

On the day of her arrival, when Clara went for her usual rest, Grandmamma sat next to her in an armchair and closed her eyes for a few minutes. Then she stood up briskly, feeling refreshed, and went into the dining room. Nobody was there, so she climbed the stairs to Miss Rottenmeyer's room and knocked sharply on the door. After a little while, the lady opened the door, shrinking back a little with surprise at the unexpected visit.

"What does the child do at this time? Where is she? That's what I want to know," said Mrs. Sesemann.

"She's in her room, where she could be doing something useful if she had the least idea how. But I have to say, Mrs. Sesemann, the kinds of things this creature gets up to can barely be mentioned in civilized society."

"Well, I have to say I think I'd be the same, if I was shut up with nothing to do. And then you'd see if you could mention what I got up to! Fetch the child and bring her to my room. I have brought some pretty picture books which I'd like to give her."

"That's just the problem," Miss Rottenmeyer cried, clasping her hands together. "What use is a book to the child? In all this time, she hasn't even learned her alphabet. It's impossible to teach this creature anything, as the tutor will tell you. If he didn't have the patience of a saint, he'd have given up trying long ago."

"That's strange. She doesn't look like a child who can't learn her alphabet," Mrs. Sesemann said. "Bring her to me. She can at least look at the pictures in the books."

Miss Rottenmeyer wanted to say something else, but Mrs. Sesemann had already turned her back and was on her way to her room. She was puzzling over the news about Heidi and was planning to investigate, though not by asking the tutor. Despite knowing him to be good natured, whenever she met him she'd say a quick hello before hurrying away in the opposite direction. She found his conversational style somewhat pedantic.

Heidi appeared in Grandmamma's room and Grandmamma began to show her one of the books. Heidi's eyes opened very wide as she gazed at the wonderful pictures. But when Grandmamma turned another page, she cried out, bright tears falling from her eyes. Grandmamma looked at the picture herself. It was of a lovely green meadow, where lots of goats and sheep were grazing. In the middle stood a goatherd, leaning on his big stick, watching over the animals. The sun was sinking low over the horizon, casting a golden shimmer over everything.

Grandmamma took Heidi's hand and said gently, "Come, come, child. Don't cry, don't cry. It must have reminded you of something. But look, there's a lovely story to go with it. I'll read it to you this evening. And there are so many more beautiful pictures in the book, all with stories to read. Come now, we have to talk about something, you and I. Dry your eyes and come and stand by me. That's right. Let's be happy again."

But it was a while before Heidi could stop sobbing. Grandmamma gave her time to recover, just saying from time to

...Grandmamma began to show her one of the books. Heidi's eyes opened very wide as she gazed at the wonderful pictures.

time, "There, there. Let's be happy again, shall we?"

When she saw that the little girl had calmed down, she said, "Now tell me, child. How are your lessons with the tutor going. Are you learning lots of things?"

"Oh, no," Heidi sighed. "But I knew already I wouldn't be able to learn anything."

"Whatever do you mean, Heidi?"

"You can't learn to read. It's just too hard."

"Oh, really? Where did you hear that?"

"Peter told me, and he knows because he's tried it over and over, and can't ever learn. It's too hard."

"But you can't just accept what any old Peter tells you. You have to try things out for yourself. Perhaps with that in your head, you've not been able to pay proper attention to the tutor or look properly at the letters of the alphabet."

"It's no use," said Heidi in a tone that suggested she was resigned to the inevitable.

"Heidi," said Grandmamma, "I have to tell you something. The reason you haven't learned anything is because you believed what this Peter told you. Well now you must believe me when I tell you in all certainty that you can learn to read very quickly, like all the other children do who are like you and not like Peter. But you have to understand what will follow if you do learn to read. You saw the goatherd on the lovely green meadow? Well, as soon as you can read, you may have that book to keep. Then you can read his story for yourself and know it just as if someone was telling it to you. You can read all about his goats and sheep and all the remarkable things that happen to him. You'd like that, wouldn't you, Heidi?"

Heidi had listened to every word and now her eyes shone and she burst out, "Oh if only I could read!"

"You will Heidi, and I can see already it won't take you long. But come now, let's go and see Clara and take the lovely books with us." And with that, she took Heidi's hand and they went into the study.

Ever since the day Heidi had tried to go home and Miss Rottenmeyer had stopped her on the stairs, something had changed for the little girl. Miss Rottenmeyer had told her it proved what a naughty, ungrateful child she was and had said it was lucky Mr. Sesemann didn't know about it, and Heidi had realized that what Aunt Dete had told her wasn't true. She wasn't free to go home whenever she liked. In fact, she had to stay in Frankfurt, for a long, long time – perhaps forever. And she gathered that Mr. Sesemann would think her ungrateful for wanting to go home, and that both Grandmamma and Clara would think the same. So she couldn't tell a soul about her wish to go back to Grandfather. If Grandmamma, who had been so kind to her, became as cross with her as Miss Rottenmeyer was, she wouldn't be able to bear it. The burden she carried in her heart grew and grew. She lost her appetite and grew a little paler every day.

At night it took her a long time to go to sleep. As soon as she was alone and everything was quiet, her head would fill with the Alm and the sunshine and the flowers, and if she finally went to sleep, she saw the red cliffs of Falknis and the fiery snowyfields of Scesaplana, and she would wake up in the morning full of joy, wanting to burst out of the Alm hut and look – but she would find herself in the big, wide bed in Frankfurt, far, far away, never to go home again. Then Heidi would press her face into the pillow and cry and cry, but quietly, so nobody would hear.

Grandmamma was quick to notice Heidi's sadness. She let a few days go by to see if things would change, but Heidi kept the same downcast manner, and some mornings Grandmamma could see that she had been crying. So one day, she took the little girl into her room and said kindly, "Tell me what's wrong, Heidi. Is something troubling you?"

But Heidi couldn't bear to tell for fear of seeming ungrateful.

"I can't tell you," she said sadly.

"No? Might you be able to tell Clara?" asked Grandmamma.

"Oh no, I can't tell anybody," said Heidi, so unhappily that Grandmamma was filled with pity.

"Come, come," said Grandmamma. "I'll tell you something. Whenever you have a secret trouble, you can always tell it to God and He will help you. You understand, don't you? Do you pray every evening to the Dear Lord, and thank Him for all your blessings, and ask Him to protect you from hardship?"

"No, never," answered the little girl.

"Have you never prayed, Heidi? Don't you know what it is?"

"I only prayed with the other Grandmother. But it's so long ago now, I've forgotten how."

"You see, Heidi, that must be why you're so sad. You don't know anyone who can help you. If you have something in your heart that causes you pain, just imagine how good it would feel to be able to go to God and tell him all about it, and ask Him to help you, and make you happy again."

Joy shone in Heidi's eyes. "Are you allowed to tell Him everything? Everything?"

"Yes, Heidi. Everything."

The little girl pulled her hand away in a hurry and said, "Please may I go?"

"Of course," replied Grandmamma. So Heidi ran straight to her room. She sat herself down on a stool, clasped her hands together and poured out her heart to God. She told him why she was so sad and begged Him to help her and let her go home to Grandfather.

About a week went by, when the tutor asked to see Mrs. Sesemann, in order to draw something curious to her attention. He was called to her room and as he came in Mrs. Sesemann offered him her hand. "My dear sir, welcome. Do sit down with me, here..." she pulled up a chair for him. "So tell me, what brings you to see me? Nothing bad, I hope?"

"Quite the opposite, my dear lady," the tutor began. "Something has happened that I could never have expected. Indeed something, given the previous evidence, that was entirely unlikely to happen, and yet really has taken place in the most wonderful way, quite contrary to..."

"Has Heidi learned to read, by any chance?" Mrs. Sesemann interjected.

The tutor gaped at her, speechless with surprise. Then he went on, "It's truly extraordinary, not only that the young girl could not learn her alphabet despite all my most thorough explanations and efforts, but that now, after I had decided to abandon all attempts to reach the unreachable goal, and simply present the girl with the letters themselves, that she has, so to speak, learned how to read overnight, and with an accuracy one rarely sees in beginners. It is just as extraordinary, however, how you, being so far removed from her lessons, could have guessed at this unlikely possibility."

"Many weird and wonderful things happen in this life," Grandmamma said, smiling with pleasure. "Sometimes two things come together by happy coincidence, such as a new enthusiasm for learning and a new method of teaching. It certainly can't hurt, my dear sir. Let's just be happy that the child has come this far, and hope she makes further progress."

With that, she showed the tutor to the door, and then rushed into the study to witness the good news for herself. Sure enough, there was Heidi sitting by Clara, reading her a story, evidently with enormous surprise at herself and growing enthusiasm as she plunged into the new world that was opening up to her, where black letters on a page came to life as people and things and touching stories.

That same evening, as she took her place at supper, Heidi found the big book with the beautiful pictures lying on her plate. When she looked questioningly at Grandmamma, the old lady nodded kindly and said, "Yes, yes. It belongs to you now."

"Forever? Even when I go home?" Heidi said, turning pink with pleasure.

"Of course. Forever," Grandmamma assured her. "We'll start reading it together tomorrow."

"But you're not going home for years yet, Heidi," Clara interjected. "When Grandmamma leaves, you have to stay here with me."

Before she went to sleep, Heidi had to look at her beautiful new book again. From that day on, she loved nothing more than sitting down with her book and reading the stories that went with the beautiful pictures. If Grandmamma said in the evening, "Heidi can read to us now," it made the little girl happy, for she found reading easy now.

The best story was the one with the picture of the goatherd in the green meadow. He looked so happy standing there, leaning on his stick, surrounded by his father's flock. But then came the picture when he had run away from his father's house. He was far from home, with a herd of pigs to look after and only a few husks of grain to eat. In this picture the sun didn't seem as golden and the land was shrouded in mist.

But there was another picture in the story, where the father was coming out of his house with outstretched arms to welcome his homecoming son. The son, all ragged and thin, was running into his arms.

Heidi never tired of reading that story. She read it over and over again, both out loud and to herself, and she loved to hear Grandmamma explain it.

There were so many more beautiful pictures in the book too, and as she looked at them, and read more stories, the days flew by, until Grandmamma's visit was nearly at an end.

Chapter Eleven

Heidi gains and loses

Every afternoon, Grandmamma would sit with Clara and close her eyes for a few moments, while Clara had her afternoon rest. Miss Rottenmeyer would disappear too, probably to relax her over-stretched nerves. But Grandmamma was soon up on her feet again. She would call Heidi into her room, and either talk to her or amuse her with little tasks. She had some pretty little dolls with her, and a cloth bag full of pieces of material. She showed Heidi how to make clothes for the dolls, and soon, without realizing it, Heidi had learned to sew and could make the prettiest little coats and dresses.

Now that Heidi could read, she often read her book of stories to Grandmamma, and the more she read them, the more she loved them. The characters began to seem like real friends who she was always glad to meet again. But Heidi never looked really happy, and the merry sparkle in her eyes had gone.

In the last week of Mrs. Sesemann's stay, Grandmamma called for Heidi, who came into the room with her big book under her arm. Grandmamma motioned for Heidi to put it down. "Now child," she said kindly. "Tell me, why aren't you happy? Is it the same trouble?"

"Yes," said Heidi.

"Have you prayed to God to help you?"

"Yes."

"And do you pray to Him every day, to let you be happy again?"

"Not any more," said Heidi.

"Why don't you pray any more? Why did you stop?"

"It didn't do any good," Heidi told her. "God didn't listen. I suppose if everyone in Frankfurt prays every evening, all at the same time, God can't listen to them all. He must have forgotten me."

"What makes you so sure?"

"I've asked every day for the same thing, for many many weeks, but God hasn't given it to me."

"But that's not how it works, Heidi. God is Father to us all, and always knows what is best for us, even though we may not know it ourselves. You see, Heidi, what you prayed for wasn't right for you just now. But God did hear you, for He can see us all and

listen to us all at once. He must have thought, 'Heidi's prayer will be answered, but only at the right moment. If I do what she asks of me now, the day will come when she will see it would have been better for me to have waited,' for things don't always turn out as we expect.

"And now, while God was looking down on you, to see if you really trusted him, and prayed to Him in your trouble, all at once you have stopped praying. You have forgotten Him and His goodness. If He doesn't hear your prayers, He will let you go your own way.

"What will you do now, Heidi? Will you go to God and pray for His forgiveness, and put your trust in Him, so He can do what is good for you, and make you happy again?"

Heidi had listened carefully, for she had great confidence in Grandmamma. And every word she said had sunk deep into her heart. "I'll go right away," she said, "and beg God's forgiveness. I'll never forget Him again."

"That is right, Heidi," Grandmamma said encouragingly, "and you may be sure He will help you when the right time comes."

And Heidi ran straight to her room and prayed that she would always remember God, and that He would not forget her.

All too soon, Grandmamma's visit came to an end. It was a sad time for Heidi and Clara, but Grandmamma made it as merry as possible until the moment she drove off in the carriage. But as soon as she had gone, silence and emptiness swept through the house. For the rest of the day Heidi and Clara sat together like two lost children, not knowing what to do with themselves.

The next day, when their lessons were over, Heidi appeared in the doorway with her big book under her arm. "Now I'll read to you, if you like, Clara?"

Clara eagerly agreed and Heidi began with enthusiasm. But hardly had she begun a new story about a sick and dying grandmother than she began to cry. "Grandmother is dead!" she sobbed. For everything she read seemed real to her, and she was sure it was the blind grandmother in Dörfli who was dying.

"I'll never see her again," she cried. "And she never even had one of those little white rolls."

Clara tried to explain that the grandmother in the story wasn't

Peter's grandmother. But even after she had convinced her, Heidi wasn't comforted. She began to worry that Grandmother might really die, when she was so far away, and Grandfather too. And that when, at last, she went back to her mountain-home, it would be silent and deserted. She would stand in front of its closed doors, knowing she would never see her loved ones again.

Miss Rottenmeyer came into the room, in time to hear Clara trying to explain things to Heidi. As Heidi went on crying, she began to look very impatient. "Adelheid," she said sternly, "that's enough. Stop this foolish crying. If I ever hear you making such a fuss again whilst reading, I'll take away the book and never give it back to you."

Heidi turned white with terror, for the book was her greatest treasure. Hastily, she dried her eyes and choked back her sobs. Miss Rottenmeyer never had to repeat her threat, for Heidi never cried again, no matter what she read. Sometimes, though, it took such an effort not to cry that Clara would exclaim, "I've never seen anything like the faces you're making."

Miss Rottenmeyer noticed nothing, however, and everything went smoothly for a while.

But Heidi had lost her appetite once more and grew so pale and thin Sebastian couldn't bear it. He began trying to tempt her with the daintiest of morsels. "Try some of this, it's excellent," he would whisper coaxingly. "Take a good spoonful. And another." But it was of no use. Heidi scarcely ate anything and when she lay down at night, she would close her eyes and see Grandfather's hut. Overcome with longing, she would bury her face in her pillow and cry until it grew wet with tears.

Time went by, and Heidi hardly knew if it were winter or summer. The high town walls always looked the same and that was all she could see from the windows of the Sesemann's house. Heidi never went outside, except when Clara was feeling well enough, and then only for a short drive. They never got beyond brick walls and stone pavements, so all Heidi saw were wide streets and handsome houses. And with each passing day, she longed more and more for grass and flowers, pine trees and mountains. Her homesickness grew, so even reading about them brought tears to her eyes, though she would not let them fall.

When summer did come, the sun shone so dazzlingly on the white walls opposite that Heidi knew the time had come when Peter would take the goats to the mountain pasture. She knew that by day the golden rockroses were glistening in the sunshine, and that in the evening everything was glowing with rosy light. Then she would sit in a lonely corner of her bedroom with both hands pressed against her eyes, trying to block out the sunshine and fighting the homesickness in her heart, until Clara sent for her again.

Chapter Twelve

The Sesemann house is haunted

Something very strange and mysterious was going on in the Sesemann house. For some days now, Miss Rottenmeyer had been going silently about the house, as if lost in thought. As dusk fell and she went from room to room, or down the long corridors, she was seen to look cautiously behind her, or peer into dark corner as if she was expecting someone to creep up behind her and tug her skirt.

She stopped going alone into some parts of the house. If she had to go to the upper floor, into the grand guest bedrooms, or worse still, to the first floor, where every step echoed in the great drawing room, she always called for Tinette to come with her, saying she might need help carrying something up or down.

Tinette began to do exactly the same, calling for Sebastian to come with her as she went about the house, in case she needed help fetching things.

Even Sebastian, when he was sent to the more distant rooms, asked Johann to accompany him. And Johann always came, even though there never was anything to carry, and either could easily have gone alone. And while all this was going on, the cook, who had been in the house for years, stood shaking her head over her pots and kettles, saying, "To think I should live to see such goings-on!"

Stranger still, every morning, when the servants went downstairs, they found the front door wide open, even though no one had opened it. The first few days this happened, every room and corner of the house was searched, for fear that something had been stolen. Everyone thought a thief must have been hiding in the house, and fled in the night with the stolen goods. But nothing in the house had been touched, and everything was safe in its place. After that, the door was double-locked at night and fastened with wooden beams. But it was no good. In the morning, it stood wide open again. And no matter how early the servants came down, full of excitement and fear, the door was always open, even though everybody around them was still fast alseep.

At last, urged on by Miss Rottenmeyer, Sebastian and Johann plucked up the courage to spend the night downstairs in the room next to the great drawing room, to wait and see what might happen. Miss Rottenmeyer gave them several of Mr. Sesemann's pistols and a bottle of spirits, to keep up their courage.

On the chosen night, they sat down with their bottle and began to drink. First they were very chatty, but in no time, they became very sleepy, so they leaned back in their armchairs and fell fast asleep.

As midnight struck, Sebastian roused himself and called to Johann, who only turned his head and slept on. Fully alert now, Sebastian listened carefully. Everything was as still as a mouse, even in the street outside. But Sebastian was too scared to go back to sleep in that ghostly silence, so he tried to rouse Johann again, shaking him gently to make him stir. At last, Johann woke up, and remembered why he was in a chair, and not his own bed. He got up and, feeling very brave, said, "Come, Sebastian, we must go outside and see what's going on. Don't be afraid, just follow me."

He opened the door and stepped into the hall. At the same

time, a sudden gust of air blew through the open front door and put out the light he held in his hand. Johann sprang back into the room, nearly knocking over Sebastian who was just behind him. He dragged Sebastian back into the room with him, slammed the door shut and turned the key as many times as it would go. Then he pulled out his matches and relit his lamp.

Sebastian hardly knew what had happened, for he hadn't seen the open door or felt the cold gust of air. But when he saw Johann's face in the lamplight, he let out a cry of alarm. Johann was as white as a ghost, and trembling all over. "What's the matter? What did you see out there?"

"The wide open door," gasped Johann, "and a white figure on the step. Then it vanished up the stairs."

Sebastian felt fear creep up his spine. The two men drew their chairs close together and sat there without stirring until morning broke, and the streets became alive again. Then they left the room together, shut the front door, and went upstairs to tell Miss Rottenmeyer what had happened. As soon as they had given her all the details, she immediately sat down and wrote to Mr. Sesemann, who had never received a letter like it in his life.

She could hardly write, she told him, for her fingers were stiff with fear. She called for Mr. Sesemann to pack his things and return home at once, for dreadful and unaccountable things were happening at home. Then she wrote all the details of what had happened – how the front door was open every morning, that no one in the house felt safe and that it was impossible to tell what terrible things might happen next.

Mr. Sesemann replied that he was quite unable to drop everything at such short notice. He found the ghost story absurd and hoped that by the time she read this letter, the ghost would have disappeared. If, however, it continued to disturb the household, would Miss Rottenmeyer please write to his mother, and ask her if she would come. He had no doubt his mother would find a way to deal with the ghost, so it wouldn't dare haunt the house again.

Miss Rottenmeyer was not pleased with the tone of this letter. She didn't think Mr. Sesemann was taking the situation seriously enough. She wrote, as asked, to Mrs. Sesemann, but did not get any more comfort from her answer. Mrs. Sesemann wrote that she had no intention of journeying all the way to Frankfurt just because Miss Rottenmeyer had thought she'd seen a ghost. There had never been a ghost in the house since she has known it, she pointed out, and if there was someone wandering around the house now, it must be a living creature, which Miss Rottenmeyer ought to be able to deal with herself. If not, she had better ask the night watchman for help.

Miss Rottenmeyer, however, was determined not to spend her days in terror any longer, and she knew exactly how to go about it. So far, she hadn't mentioned anything about the ghost to the children, for she knew if she did, the children wouldn't want to be left alone for an instant, which would give her a great deal of trouble. But now she went straight to the study, and there, in a low whisper, told them of the mysterious nightly visitor.

"I can't be left alone!" declared Clara immediately. "Father must come home, and Miss Rottenmeyer, you must sleep in my room. Heidi can't be left alone either, in case the ghost should do anything to her. We'll all sleep together in one room and keep a light burning all night. Perhaps Tinette had better be in the room next to us, and Sebastian and Johann can spend the night in the hall, so they can frighten away the ghost as soon as it appears."

Clara grew so excited that Miss Rottenmeyer had great difficulty calming her. She promised to write at once to her father and to move her bed into Clara's room. "We can't all sleep in the same room," she went on, "but if Heidi is frightened, Tinette can go into her room."

Heidi was far more frightened of Tinette than of ghosts, which she'd never even heard of before. She promised the others she wasn't in the least afraid of the ghost, and would much rather be left alone at night.

Miss Rottenmeyer now sat down to write another letter to Mr. Sesemann, letting him know that the mysterious happenings about the house were beginning to affect his daughter's delicate health. That helped. Two days later, Mr. Sesemann stood at his front door and rang the bell so forcefully, everybody came rushing from all parts of the house, convinced the ghost had become bolder, and was now playing its tricks in the daytime. Sebastian peered cautiously through the half-closed shutters, and just as he did so there came another violent ring at the bell, which was impossible to mistake for anything other than a man's hand. Recognizing whose hand it was, Sebastian came rushing out of the room, fell head over heels downstairs, picked himself up and flung open the street door.

Mr. Sesemann hardly noticed him, and raced straight up the stairs to his daughter's room. Clara greeted him with a cry of joy and Mr. Sesemann's face cleared of anxiety as he heard from his daughter's own lips that she was as well as ever. "I am almost glad about the ghost, Father," she said, "if it's made you come home again."

"And how are things with the ghost?" he asked, turning to Miss Rottenmeyer, with a twinkle of amusement in his eye.

"It is no joking matter, I assure you," replied Miss Rottenmeyer. "You'll not be laughing tomorrow morning. These nightly visits suggest something terrible must have happened here in the past. Something terrible that has never been revealed... until now!"

"Well I don't know anything about that," said Mr. Sesemann cheerfully. "But I hope you aren't suspecting my worthy ancestors. And now, will you kindly call Sebastian into the dining room, as I wish to speak to him alone." He had noticed that Sebastian and Miss Rottenmeyer were far from being the best of friends, and it had given him his own suspicions about the ghost.

"Come here," he said, as soon as Sebastian appeared. "Tell me honestly, have you been pretending to be ghosts to scare Miss Rottenmeyer?"

"No, no, I promise, sir," said Sebastian. "You mustn't think that. I've been very worried about the ghost myself."

"Well then, I'll just have to show you and Johann what ghosts look like by daylight. You ought to be ashamed of yourself! A strong man like you shouldn't be running away from ghosts. Now, take my compliments to my old friend, the doctor, and ask him to meet me without fail at nine o' clock this evening. Tell him I've come all the way from Paris to consult him, and that he must come prepared to wait up all night. Have you got that?"

"Certainly, sir! I'll deliver the message at once."

Mr. Sesemann then went back to comfort Clara, telling her she shouldn't worry any more about the ghost, as he was about to put an end to it.

On the dot of nine, with the children in bed and Miss Rottenmeyer retired for the night, the doctor arrived. He was fresh-faced, with bright, kindly eyes. He looked anxious as he walked in, but as soon as he saw Mr. Sesemann he clapped him on the shoulder and laughed. "Well, well! You look pretty well for a man wanting someone to sit up with him all night."

"Not so fast, old friend, not so fast," retorted Mr. Sesemann. "The one you have to sit up for will look a good deal worse once we have caught him."

"So there's a sick person in the house... that must be caught?"

"Worse than that, doctor. There's a ghost in the house!"

The doctor burst out laughing.

"Where's your sympathy? It's a pity Miss Rottenmeyer isn't here to enjoy it. She's convinced that an ancient Sesemann is wandering the house doing penance for a terrible crime."

"How did she come to meet the ghost?" asked the doctor, still chuckling.

Mr. Sesemann told his friend the whole story, adding, "To be on the safe side, I've loaded two pistols and put them in the room where we're to spend the night. Either this is some joke by one of the servants' friends, in which case a shot in the air will give them a well-deserved fright, or there are thieves about, trying to keep the servants to their rooms so they can plunder the house in peace. If that's the case, it'll be no bad thing if we're armed."

By now, the two gentlemen had reached the room where Johann and Sebastian had spent the night. On the table stood some bottles of good wine for refreshment, two pistols and a couple of candlesticks, shining brightly. Mr. Sesemann had no intention of waiting for the ghost in semi-darkness.

The door was nearly closed, so that no light could escape and frighten the ghost away. Then the gentlemen settled themselves comfortably in the armchairs and found so much to talk about, between glasses of wine, that they couldn't believe it when the clock struck twelve.

"The ghost's got wind of us and is keeping away," said the doctor.

"Patience, friend, patience!" replied Mr. Sesemann. "They say it doesn't come until one o' clock."

They started talking again until one o' clock struck. There wasn't a sound in the house or even in the street outside. Suddenly, the doctor raised a finger.

"Hush, Sesemann! Do you hear something?"

They both listened, and distinctly heard the bar of the door being pushed aside. Then the key turned in the lock and the front door creaked open. Moonlight crept into the house. There was silence for a moment, then the sound of footsteps quietly going up the stairs.

Mr. Sesemann reached for his pistol.

"You aren't afraid, are you?" asked the doctor.

"It's better to be careful," Mr. Sesemann whispered back. They each took a light in one hand, and a pistol in the other, and went softly to the door and out into the hall.

There, on the stairs, in the flickering shadows, stood a small motionless figure.

"Who's there?" thundered the doctor.

His voice echoed down the corridors, as the two men advanced towards the figure, clutching their lights and their weapons.

The figure turned and gave a low cry. In bare feet, dressed

in her white nightgown, Heidi gazed at them with dazed eyes, trembling and shaking like a leaf in the wind.

"Why, it's your little water-carrier!" exclaimed the doctor.

"Child, what are you doing here?" asked Mr. Sesemann. "Why did you come down?"

"I don't know," whispered Heidi, her face white with terror.

The doctor stepped forward. "I think this is a matter for me to see to, Sesemann. Go back to your chair and I'll take this child up to bed."

He put his pistol on the floor, took Heidi by the hand and went towards the stairs. "Don't be afraid," he said cheerfully as they went up. "There's nothing to be frightened about."

When they reached Heidi's room, he set his light on the table and lifted Heidi into bed, carefully tucking in the sheets around her. Then he sat down beside her and waited until she had grown a little calmer. Taking Heidi's hand in his, he said soothingly, "There, now you feel better, tell me where you wanted to go?"

"I didn't want to go anywhere," Heidi replied. "I didn't even know I'd gone downstairs. I was just there."

"And did you dream about anything during the night?"

"Oh yes, I always dream the same dream, every night. I think I am back at Grandfather's, and I hear the sound of the wind in the pine trees, and I see the stars shining brightly. Then I open the door quickly and run out, and it's all so beautiful! But when I wake up I'm still in Frankfurt." A lump came to her throat and she

In bare feet, dressed in her white nightgown, Heidi gazed at them with dazed eyes, trembling and shaking like a leaf in the wind.

tried to swallow it.

"Have you any pain anywhere?" asked the doctor. "In your head or back?"

"No, only a feeling as if there were a great stone weighing on me here." Heidi pointed to her chest.

"As if you'd eaten something that wouldn't go down?"

"No, not like that. It's a heavy feeling, like wanting to cry."

"I see. And then, do you have a good cry?"

"Oh no, I mustn't. Miss Rottenmeyer has forbidden it."

"So you swallow it down, do you? Have you been happy here in Frankfurt?"

"Yes," whispered Heidi, but it sounded more like the opposite.

"And where did you live with your grandfather?"

"Up on the mountain."

"Really! That doesn't sound much fun. Wasn't it rather dull?"

"Oh no! It's so beautiful." Heidi couldn't say anything more. Just remembering it all, the fright downstairs and the pent up tears... it was suddenly too much for her. The tears rushed to her eyes and she broke into loud, choking sobs.

"Go on crying," said the doctor, kindly. "It will do you good. Afterwards, you must try to sleep. Everything will be all right in the morning."

Then he left the room and went downstairs. "Sesemann," he said, "let me first tell you that Heidi is sleepwalking. She is the ghost who has opened the door each night and terrified your servants. Secondly, she is homesick. She is so consumed with longing to go home she is not much more than skin and bone. Something must be done at once. For her nerves and her longing, there is only one cure – to send her back home tomorrow. That is my only prescription."

Mr. Sesemann had risen to his feet and began to pace the room in distress. "What!" he cried. "You're asking me to send this child back to her grandfather as a miserable little skeleton, when she came here happy and healthy? I can't do it. Look after the child, do everything you can for her, and then she shall go home. But do something first."

"Sesemann," replied the doctor, "think about what you are saying. Heidi's illness cannot be cured with pills and powders. She's not robust, but if you send her home now she'll soon be herself again. If not – wouldn't you rather she went back ill than not at all?"

Mr. Sesemann stopped in shock. "If you put it like that, doctor, of course Heidi must go home, and go at once."

Then he and the doctor walked up and down for a little while, talking it over thoroughly and arranging what to do. When Mr. Sesemann at last opened the front door to let his friend out, the morning light was shining in.

Chapter Thirteen

A summer evening on the mountain

Feeling anxious and agitated, Mr. Sesemann went upstairs and knocked loudly on Miss Rottenmeyer's door. She gave a cry of alarm. "Hurry!" he called, waking her from her sleep. "Come down to the dining room. Preparations must be made for a journey."

Miss Rottenmeyer looked at her clock. It said half past four. She had never been up so early in her life. What could have happened? She rushed to put on her clothes, and in her haste kept searching for clothes she had already put on.

Meanwhile, Mr. Sesemann had gone through the hall, ringing all the servants' bells to call them from their rooms. Each leaped from their beds, terrified the ghost had attacked their master in the night and that he was calling for help.

One by one, they appeared in the dining room, each looking more terrified than the last. They were astonished to see Mr. Sesemann cheerfully walking up and down, not looking as if he'd just seen a ghost at all.

Johann was sent at once to get the horse and carriage ready, Tinette was ordered to wake Heidi and get her dressed for her journey. Sebastian hurried off to the house where Dete worked, with orders to bring her back with him. Then Miss Rottenmeyer, who had at last finished getting ready, came down with her cap on the wrong way round. From a distance, it looked as if she were walking backwards. Mr. Sesemann rightly put this down to her early start, and immediately began giving her directions. "Get out a trunk for Heidi and pack up all her belongings," he ordered. "Pack some of Clara's clothes too, for I want her to have plenty of clothes to take home. This must be done immediately."

Miss Rottenmeyer could only stare in astonishment. She'd expected to learn all about his terrible experience with the ghost, which she was quite looking forward to hearing in daylight. Instead, there were these troublesome directions. She couldn't understand it, and stood waiting for more of an explanation.

But Mr. Sesemann had no thought or time for explanations. He left her standing there while he went to speak to Clara. As he had guessed, she had been woken by all the noise in the house, and was wondering what had happened. So he sat down and told her the events of the night. "The doctor says Heidi is in a very delicate state. The ghost wasn't a ghost but Heidi sleepwalking. Her nightly wandering could become dangerous," he finished. "She might even climb onto the roof. And so we've decided to send her home at once. You must see that it's the only thing to do."

Clara was deeply upset and begged her father to change his mind, coming up with all sorts of suggestions of how they might keep Heidi. But her father was firm, and promised her that if she didn't make a fuss, he would take her to Switzerland next summer.

At last she gave in, only begging that Heidi's trunk could be brought into her room, so she could add whatever she liked as presents for Heidi. Her father happily agreed.

Downstairs, Dete had arrived and was waiting in the hall, wondering what extraordinary thing could have happened for her to be called upon so early. Mr. Sesemann explained how it was with Heidi and that he wished for Dete to take her home that very day.

Dete thought with dread of the Alm Uncle's last words, that he wished never to set eyes on her again. She *couldn't* take Heidi back to him like this, not after the way she'd carried her off. It was too much to ask of her.

"It's quite impossible," she said to Mr. Sesemann. "I can't take off today or tomorrow as I have far too much to do. I doubt I can get away any day this week."

Mr. Sesemann guessed she was reluctant to go and dismissed her without another word. Then he sent for Sebastian and told him to get ready to go. He was to travel with Heidi as far as Basel, spend the night there, and then take her home the following day. He would give him a letter to give to Heidi's grandfather, which would explain everything.

"But there is one very important thing I want you to remember," added Mr. Sesemann. "I know the people who run this hotel in Basel. Here is a card with their names. They'll give you and Heidi a room for the night. When you get there, make sure that all of the windows in Heidi's room are securely fastened, and after Heidi is in bed, lock her bedroom door on the outside. She walks in her sleep which could easily be dangerous for her in a strange house."

"Oh! So that was it!" exclaimed Sebastian, suddenly understanding what lay behind the ghost.

"Yes, that was it! You've been a fool and you may tell Johann he's been one too." And with that, Mr. Sesemann went to his study to write a letter to the Alm Uncle.

Sebastian was left feeling shamefaced. "If only I hadn't let Johann drag me back into the room. If only I'd gone after that little figure in white."

Meanwhile, Heidi was standing in her Sunday frock, waiting to see what would happen next. Tinette had woken her with a shake and had put on her clothes without uttering a word. She thought Heidi far too beneath her notice to speak to her.

Mr. Sesemann went back to the dining room with the letter, by which time breakfast was ready. "Where's the child?" he asked.

Heidi was quickly fetched. She came into the dining room and gave him her usual "Good morning."

"What do you say to this, little one?" Mr. Sesemann asked her. Heidi only looked at him wonderingly.

"Has nobody told you?" laughed Mr. Sesemann. "You are going home today!"

"Home?" murmured Heidi, turning pale. For a moment she could hardly breathe.

"Aren't you pleased?"

"Oh yes! I am, I am!" cried Heidi, her cheeks blushing red.

"Good, good," said Mr. Sesemann, sitting down, and motioning for Heidi to do the same. "Now have a good breakfast, and then you can go off in the carriage."

But Heidi couldn't even manage a mouthful. She was far too excited, and hardly knew if she were awake or dreaming, or if she would open her eyes again and find herself in her nightgown at the front door.

"The child can't eat a thing now, completely understandably. Tell Sebastian to take plently of food with him," Mr. Sesemann called to Miss Rottenmeyer, who had just come into the room. He turned to Heidi, adding kindly, "Now run up to Clara and stay with her till the carriage arrives."

Heidi had been longing for this, and ran quickly out of the room. A huge trunk was standing right in the middle of Clara's room.

"Look, Heidi! See what we've packed in your trunk," Clara called out. "There are dresses and aprons, shawls and sewing things. I do hope you like them. And see here," she added, holding up a little basket in triumph. Heidi peered in and jumped for joy. Inside were at least a dozen beautiful white rolls, all for Grandmother. In their delight, the children forgot that they were about to part, and when someone called out, "The carriage is here!" there was no time for grieving.

Heidi ran to her room to fetch her book – her beautiful book that Grandmamma had given her. It was under her pillow, where she always kept it, for she could never bear to be parted from it. She put it in her basket with the rolls. Then she looked in her cupboard, and just as she had thought, there was her old everyday dress and red shawl. Miss Rottenmeyer had not thought it was good enough to pack along with the other things. Heidi wrapped the dress and scarf around her beloved book and placed the bundle on top of the basket. Then she put on a pretty dress and hat and left the room.

Heidi and Clara had little time to say goodbye, for Mr. Sesemann was waiting to put Heidi into her carriage and Miss Rottenmeyer was standing at the top of the stairs to say farewell. When she caught sight of the red bundle, she snatched it out of the basket and threw it to the ground. "No, Adelheid!" she exclaimed. "I forbid you to leave the house with that thing. Goodbye." Heidi didn't dare pick up her bundle again, she could only gaze imploringly at Mr. Sesemann, as if she were losing her greatest treasure.

"Heidi can take home whatever she wants," said Mr. Sesemann, decidedly. "Even kittens and tortoises if it pleases her."

Heidi quickly picked up the bundle, giving Mr. Sesemann a look brimming with gratitude. Mr. Sesemann shook her hand. "I hope you will remember Clara and me," he said.

"Thank you, for all your kindness," Heidi replied. "And please say goodbye to the doctor for me, and thank him." She had not forgotten that he'd promised that everything would be all right in the morning, and she guessed he must have helped this come true.

Now Heidi was lifted into the carriage, the basket and

provisions were put in, and finally Sebastian climbed in too.

"Goodbye," Mr. Sesemann called, as the carriage rolled away.

Very soon, Heidi was sitting on the train, clutching her basket tightly because of the precious rolls inside. Every now and then she peered at them with satisfaction. She sat in silence, growing more and more excited, realizing she really was going home to Grandfather and the mountain, to Peter and Grandmother. And as they all rose as images before her eyes, another thought struck her. "Sebastian," she said anxiously, "are you sure that Grandmother is still alive?"

"Yes," mumbled Sebastian, half-asleep. "I'm sure she's alive. There's no reason why she should be dead."

After a little while, Heidi fell asleep too, and didn't wake until Sebastian shook her by the arm. "Wake up! Wake up!" he called. "We have to get out. We're at Basel."

The next day, there was another train journey lasting many hours. Heidi sat again with her basket on her knee, for she could never let Sebastian take it, even for a moment. She was too excited to talk, and her excitement increased every mile that passed. Then suddenly, before Heidi expected it, a voice called out 'Mayenfeld!'

Both Heidi and Sebastian jumped up and in another minute they were standing on the platform with Heidi's trunk, and the train was steaming away down the valley. Sebastian looked after it regretfully, reluctant to begin the tiring climb. He was sure it would be dangerous too, and that the countryside was wild and savage. He looked cautiously about, to see if there was anyone he could ask for the safest way to Dörfli. Just outside the station, he saw a shabby little horse and cart, which a man was loading with heavy sacks from the train. Sebastian asked his question.

"All the roads are safe," said the man, curtly.

"And which is the best way to go, to avoid falling off the precipices? And do you know how I can get this trunk to Dörfli?"

The man looked over at the trunk. "I can take it in my own cart," he said, "as I'm driving to Dörfli."

After that, it was agreed that the man should take both Heidi and the trunk to Dörfli, and there find someone to take Heidi up the mountain.

"I can go by myself," said Heidi, who had been listening to the conversation. "I know the way from Dörfli."

Sebastian was relieved at the thought of escaping the climb up the mountain. He drew Heidi aside and gave her a thick rolled parcel and a letter for her grandfather. "The parcel is a present from Mr. Sesemann. You must put it at the bottom of your basket, under the rolls and be very careful not to lose it. Mr. Sesemann would be very cross if you did."

"I won't lose it," said Heidi, confidently, putting it with the letter at the bottom of her basket.

By now, the trunk had been lifted onto the cart. Sebastian lifted Heidi and her basket onto the high seat and shook hands with her. Then he motioned for her to keep her eye on the basket.

He was feeling guilty, knowing he ought really to have seen Heidi safely home himself.

The driver swung himself up beside Heidi and the cart rolled away towards the mountain. Relieved, Sebastian sat down and waited for his train.

The driver of the cart was the baker from Dörfli, who was taking home his sacks of flour. He had never seen Heidi before, but like everyone in Dörfli he knew all about her. He was sure this was the girl he had heard so much about, and he began to wonder why she had come back.

"You're the child who lived with the Alm Uncle, aren't you?" he began.

"Yes."

"Why have you come back from Frankfurt so soon? Were they unkind to you?"

"It wasn't that. Everyone was very kind to me."

"Then why are you coming home again?"

"Mr. Sesemann said I could come."

"Weren't you better off in Frankfurt than at home? Why didn't you want to stay there?"

"I'd rather be with Grandfather on the mountain than anywhere else in the world."

"Perhaps you'll think differently when you get back there," grumbled the baker. He said no more and began to whistle, while Heidi looked around, filled with excitement. She knew every tree along the way, and the high, jagged peaks of the mountain looked down on her like old friends. She felt wild with longing and wanted to jump down from the cart and run as fast as she could, all the way home. But she kept all her excitement inside her and sat quite still.

The clock struck five as they drove into Dörfli. Immediately a crowd of women and children surrounded the cart, curious to know who was inside the cart and where they were going.

As the baker lifted Heidi down, she said quickly, "Thank you! Grandfather will send for the trunk." She tried to run off, but the people in the crowd caught hold of her and began pestering her with questions. Heidi pushed her way through them, and seeing her distress they let her go.

"You see how frightened she is," they said to each other. "And no wonder, if she's going to the Alm Uncle." They chattered about how much worse he had grown last year, never speaking a word, always looking so furious. "Surely the child can have nowhere else to go, or she wouldn't run back to that dragon's den."

Here the baker interrupted them. "I know more about it than you do," he said. "A kind gentleman brought her to Mayenfeld and paid me to take her without any bargaining. What's more, the child said she'd had everything she wanted in Frankfurt, and that it was her own wish to go back to her grandfather."

This news, greeted with surprise, was soon repeated all over Dörfli. That evening, there wasn't a house that didn't know that

Heidi had come back, of her own accord, to her grandfather.

Heidi climbed up the steep path from Dörfli as quickly as she could. She had to pause every now and then to take a breath, for her basket was heavy and the path became steeper as she neared the top. Heidi only had one thought: "Would Grandmother be sitting in the corner by her spinning wheel? Oh! Would she still be alive?"

At last she caught sight of Grandmother's house and her heart began to beat faster. She broke into a run, but when she reached the house she was trembling so much she could hardly open the door. Then she was standing inside, too breathless to say a word.

"Oh!" came a voice from the corner. "That was how Heidi used to run in. If only I could have her with me again. Who's there?"

"I'm here, Grandmother. I'm here!" Heidi ran to the old woman and flung herself down, seizing Grandmother's hands and clinging to her, unable to speak she was so happy. And Grandmother couldn't say a word either, but stroked Heidi's soft hair and said, "Yes, this is her hair, and her voice. Thank you God for answering my prayers." Tears fell from her blind eyes onto Heidi's hand. "Is it really you, Heidi? Have you really come back?"

"Yes, I am really here, Grandmother," said Heidi. "Don't cry, for I have come back and I'm never going away again. I'll come and see you every day, and you won't have to eat any more black bread for a while. Here!"

And Heidi took the rolls from the basket and piled them, one after the other, onto Grandmother's lap.

"Ah, child! What a lovely present to bring me!" said Grandmother, her fingers running over the rolls. "But you are the best present of all," she added, stroking Heidi's hot cheeks. "Say something, so that I can hear your voice."

"I've been so unhappy, worrying that you would die when I was away. And then I'd never be able to give you the white rolls, and never, never see you again."

At that moment, Peter's mother came in, and stood staring at Heidi in astonishment. "It's Heidi!" she exclaimed. "How can that be?"

Heidi rose and shook hands with Brigitte, who looked admiringly at all her clothes. "Oh, Mother!" she said. "If you could only see the beautiful dress she has on. I scarcely recognized her! And the hat on the table, with the feather in it! Is that yours too? Do put it on, so I can see you in it."

"No, I don't want it," said Heidi. "I have a hat of my own. You can have it if you like." She hadn't forgotten how Grandfather had told Dete that he never wished to see her feathered hat again.

"Don't be so foolish," said Brigitte. "If you don't want the hat, you must sell it in Dörfli. You could get good money for it."

Heidi hid the hat quietly in a corner, took off her pretty dress and put on her old one. Then she clasped Grandmother's hands. "I must go home to Grandfather," she said. "But I'll come again tomorrow. Good night, Grandmother."

"Oh yes! Do come tomorrow," begged Grandmother, still

clutching Heidi's hands, unwilling to let her go.

At last she did, and Brigitte went with Heidi to the door. "Be careful, Heidi," she said in a whisper. "Peterkin tells me the Alm Uncle is always in a bad temper now and never says a word to him. And why have you taken off your pretty dress?" she asked.

"Because I'd rather go home to Grandfather as I am, or he might not know me. You said you hardly recognized me at first."

Then Heidi wished Brigitte good night and carried on up the mountain, her basket on her arm. All around her, the green slopes shone in the evening sun. Shining, snow-covered Scesaplana rose into view. Heidi had to stop every few steps and look back at it. And there were the two high peaks of Falknis, rising into the air like flames, with rose-tinted clouds floating above. The whole valley below was bathed in a golden mist. Heidi had forgotten how beautiful it was, and as she gazed tears ran down her cheeks. "Thank you God for bringing me home," she said out loud. But she couldn't find any more words to thank Him.

Only when the brilliance of the sunset began to fade could she tear herself away, and then she ran so quickly that very soon she saw the tops of the pine trees, and the roof of the hut itself and at last the whole hut. And there was Grandfather, sitting outside on his bench, smoking his pipe. Before he had time to see her coming, Heidi rushed up to him, dropped her basket and flung her arms around his neck. "Grandfather! Grandfather! Grandfather!" she said over and over again.

The old man said nothing. For the first time in many years he had tears in his eyes. He brushed them away with his hand, loosened her arms from his neck and placed her on his knee. He looked at her for a moment, then said, "So you've come back to me, Heidi? How did that happen? You don't look like a grand lady. Did they send you away?"

"Oh no, Grandfather, you mustn't think that. They were all so kind – Clara and Grandmamma and Mr. Sesemann. It was just that I couldn't bear being away from you. I thought I would die, for I felt I couldn't breathe. But I never said anything as it would have been ungrateful. And then one morning, quite early, Mr. Sesemann told me – and I think it was partly the doctor's doing – Oh! Perhaps it's all in the letter!" Heidi jumped down and fetched the parcel and the letter and handed them both to her grandfather.

"That belongs to you," said Grandfather, taking a roll of money from the parcel and puting it on the bench beside her. Then he read the letter and put it in his pocket without another word.

"Would you like some milk?" he asked, taking Heidi's hand and leading her towards the hut. "Bring your money with you. You can buy a bed and some more clothes with it. At least enough for a couple more years."

"I don't want it," replied Heidi. "I've got a bed already and Clara's given me such a lot of clothes, I won't ever need any more."

"Fetch it and put it in the cupboard. You never know, you might want it one day."

Heidi obeyed. She looked eagerly around the hut, then went up the ladder. There was a pause. "Oh, Grandfather," she called. "My bed's gone."

"We can soon make it up again," he answered. "I didn't know you were coming back. Come now and have your milk."

Heidi sat down on her high stool and drained her mug as if she'd never had anything more delicious in her life. "Our milk tastes nicer than anything else in the world, Grandfather."

There was a shrill whistle outisde and Heidi darted out to see Peter coming down the path with the goats. When he saw Heidi he gazed at her speechlessly.

"Good evening, Peter," called Heidi, before running to the goats. "Little Swan! Little Bear! Do you remember me?"

The goats recognized her voice and began rubbing their heads against her and bleating loudly. Then she called the other goats by name and they all came scampering towards her. Goldfinch leaped over the others to get nearer and even shy little Snowflake butted Bullfinch out of the way.

Heidi was delighted to be with her old friends again. She patted them and stroked them and they nudged her affectionately, until at last she came to where Peter was standing.

"Aren't you going to say hello?" she asked.

Peter found his voice again at last. "So you're back?" he said. "Will you come out with me tomorrow?"

"Not tomorrow, but I will the day after, for I must go and see

Grandmother tomorrow."

"I'm glad you're back," said Peter, and his whole face lit up as he smiled. Then he tried to go on with the goats, but he had more trouble with them than ever before. When at last he'd gathered them altogether, and Heidi had taken Little Swan and Little Bear to their stall, they suddenly turned and ran after her. Heidi had to go into the stall and the shut the door, before Peter was able to take his goats down the mountain.

When Heidi came indoors again she found her bed piled high with delicious-smelling hay. Grandfather had carefully spread it over the floor and tucked in the clean sheets. Heidi lay down and slept more soundly than she had for a year.

Grandfather got up at least ten times that night and climbed the ladder to make sure Heidi was all right, and to check the hay he had stuffed into the round window was keeping the moonlight from shining too brightly on her. But Heidi did not stir. Her heart was satisfied. She had seen the sunset on the mountains. She had heard the wind sighing through the pine trees. She was home again at last.

Chapter Fourteen

When the church bells ring

Heidi stood beneath the waving pine trees, waiting for Grandfather. He was going to Dörfli to fetch her trunk while she visited Grandmother. She could hardly wait to see Grandmother again and find out how the rolls had tasted. But she didn't mind waiting, as long as she could listen to the familiar sound of the wind in the trees and gaze at the green mountain pastures.

At last, Grandfather came out of the hut. "We can go now," he said in a cheerful voice. It was Saturday, the day he tidied the whole house, inside and out. He'd been busy all morning, so he could go with Heidi in the afternoon.

They parted at Grandmother's hut and Heidi ran in.

"Is it you, child? Have you come again?" cried Grandmother, as soon as she heard her steps.

Grandmother clasped Heidi's hand and held it tightly, as if afraid she might be taken from her again.

"Did you like the rolls?" asked Heidi.

"They were delicious. I feel stronger today than I have for a long time."

"Mother's so afraid of finishing them, she's only had one roll," added Brigitte. "But I'm sure she'd grow quite strong again if she had one a day for a week."

Heidi listened very carefully to what Brigitte said, and sat thinking for a while.

"I know what I'll do!" she said eagerly. "I'll write to Clara and ask her for more rolls. Perhaps she'll send twice as many. For I had a large heap of them in my wardrobe, but they were taken away, and Clara promised to give me as many back, and I'm sure she'll do it."

"That's a good idea," said Brigitte, "but they would get hard and stale. The baker in Dörfli makes white rolls, but I can only just manage to pay for the black bread we eat."

"Oh! But I have lots of money, Grandmother," cried Heidi, dancing around the room. "And now I know just what I'll do with it! You must have a fresh white roll every day, and two on Sundays. Peter can bring them home with him from Dörfli."

"No, no, child," said Grandmother. "I can't let you do that. The money was meant for you. Give it to Grandfather and he will tell you how to spend it."

But Heidi was determined. "Now Grandmother will have a roll a day," she said over and over, "and grow strong again – and, oh, Grandmother!" she exclaimed suddenly. "If you get strong perhaps you'll be able to see again."

Grandmother said nothing, not wanting to spoil Heidi's pleasure. As Heidi skipped around the room, she suddenly caught sight of Grandmother's song book, and that gave her another idea. "I can read now, Grandmother. Would you like me to read you a hymn from your old book?"

"Oh yes," said Grandmother, delighted. "Can you really read?"

Heidi had climbed onto a chair and was already lifting down the book, bringing a cloud of dust with it. She wiped it clean, and sat down on a stool beside Grandmother. "Which hymn would you like me to read?" she asked.

"Anything you please," Grandmother replied. She pushed her spinning-wheel to one side and waited eagerly.

Heidi turned over the pages, reading a line here and there to herself. "Here's one about the sun," she said at last. "I'll read it to you."

Grandmother listened with her hands folded in her lap and tears running down her cheeks, although Heidi had never seen her so happy.

"Oh, read the last part again, Heidi," she said.

Heidi did so, enjoying them as much as Grandmother.

After the churning seas
And the howling storm
Comes the gentle breeze
And the shining sun

All our sorrows will cease
And we will find rest
There'll be joy and peace
In God's garden blest

"What happiness you've brought me," said Grandmother at last. "I can't tell you how you've lightened my heart."

Heidi couldn't take her eyes from Grandmother's face. It didn't look troubled anymore, but filled with peace.

Then came a knock at the window, and Heidi looked up to see Grandfather beckoning to her.

"I promise I'll come and see you tomorrow," said Heidi. "Even if I go out with Peter, I'll only spend half the day with him." The thought of making Grandmother happy again gave her great pleasure, greater even than being out on the mountain with the flowers and the goats.

As she left, Brigitte ran to her with the dress and hat she'd left behind. Heidi put the dress over her arm, but she refused to take back the hat.

"You can keep it," she said to Brigitte. "I'll never wear it again."

Then she began to tell Grandfather all about her morning, about the white rolls and how they'd made Grandmother feel stronger. "If Grandmother won't take the money, will you give it to me, so I can give Peter enough to buy a roll a day, and two on Sunday?"

"What about your bed?" asked Grandfather. "Wouldn't you like a proper bed, and there would be plenty of money left over for the bread?"

"But I sleep much better on my hay bed than I ever did in Frankfurt on a proper bed. Please let me pay for the rolls, Grandfather."

"The money is yours to do as you wish with it," he said at last. "You can buy bread for Grandmother for as long as you want."

"Oh Grandfather," said Heidi, taking hold of his hand, "everything is happier now that it has ever been before." Then she grew quiet again. "If God had let me come home at once, as I asked, then everything would have been different. I would only have had a little bread to give to Grandmother, and I wouldn't have been able to read to her. But God arranged everything, just as Grandmamma said he would. I'm so glad God didn't let me have everything I prayed for at once. And now I shall always pray to God, just like she told me, and thank Him. And when He doesn't do something I ask for, I'll think it is just like in Frankfurt, and that He will do something better still. So we'll pray every day, won't we, Grandfather? And we'll never forget Him again, or else He may forget us."

"And what if someone does forget Him?" asked Grandfather, in a low voice.

"Then everything goes wrong," said Heidi, "for God lets you go your own way. And no one pities you. They just say, you ran away from God when He could have helped you."

"That's true, Heidi. Where did you learn that?"

"From Grandmamma. She explained it all to me."

Grandfather walked on for a little while without speaking. "No one can go back," he said at last. "Once God has forgotten you, you are forgotten forever."

"Oh no! We can go back. Grandmamma told me that too. And it says so in the story in my book. But you haven't heard it yet. Let's go home and I'll read it to you, and you can see how beautiful it is."

And in her hurry she let go of Grandfather's hand and raced into the hut. Grandfather put down his basket, in which he'd carried part of the contents of Heidi's trunk, which was too heavy to carry up as it was. Then he sat down on the bench outside and began thinking.

Heidi soon came running out with her book under her arm. It fell open at the right page, she'd looked at it so often, and she began to read. "There was a shepherd," she began, "who was happy at home. Every day he would go out into the fields with his father's flock until the sun went down. But then he began to long for fine things and to be his own master. So he asked for his share of his father's fortune and left home. But in no time, he had wasted it all. When he had nothing left, he had to hire himself out as a swineherd and watch over someone else's pigs. His clothes had turned to rags and he had only a few husks of grain to eat. Then he thought of his old happy life at home, and his kind father, and how ungrateful he'd been, and he wept with sorrow and longing. 'I'll go to my father. I'll tell him I don't deserve to be his son. I'll ask him to make me one of his hired servants.'

"He set off for home, but when he was still a great way off, his father saw him...

"What do you think happens now, Grandfather?" asked Heidi. "Do you think his father will say 'I told you so?' Well, listen to what comes next.

"His father saw him, and forgave him and threw his arms around him. 'I've sinned, Father,' said the young man. 'I'm not worthy of being your son.' But the father told his servants to bring out the best cloak and to put it on him. And to put a ring on his hand and shoes on his feet and to bring out the fattest calf and kill it so they could feast and be merry. 'My son was dead, but now he is alive again. He was lost and now he is found.'

"Isn't that a beautiful story?" said Heidi, as her Grandfather sat in silence.

"You're right. It's a beautiful tale," he replied. But he still looked so grave that Heidi said nothing more, but sat looking quietly at the pictures. After a while, she gently put the book on her Grandfather's lap. "See how happy he is there," she said, pointing to a picture of the son, back in his home again, standing next to his father.

A few hours later, as Heidi lay fast asleep in her bed, her grandfather went up the ladder with his lamp. He looked at Heidi as she slept, her hands folded, as if she'd fallen asleep saying her prayers, her expression full of trust and peace. He stood for a long time, gazing down at her. Then he folded his hands and said in a low voice, "God, I have sinned. I am not worthy to be called your son." And two large tears rolled down his cheeks.

Early the next morning, Grandfather stood in front of his hut and gazed around him. A few early bells rung up from the valley and the birds were singing in the pine trees. He went back into the hut. "Come along, Heidi!" he called. "The sun is up! Put on your best dress. We're going to church together."

Heidi quickly got ready. She put on her pretty Frankfurt dress and came down. "Grandfather!" she cried. "I've never seen you look like that before! You look so grand in your Sunday best!"

Grandfather smiled. "And so do you," he replied. "Now come along." He took Heidi's hand and together they walked down the mountain. As they neared the valley the bells rang louder, from every direction. "Listen!" cried Heidi. "It's like a festival."

The congregation had begun singing when Heidi and

Grandfather entered the church at Dörfli, and sat down at the back. But before the hymn was over a whisper was going about the congregation. "Do you see? The Alm Uncle is in church!"

Some of the women kept turning around to look at him and lost their place in the hymn. But when the sermon began they turned back again, for the pastor spoke with such warmth and thanksgiving his listeners were filled with joy. When the service had finished, the Alm Uncle took Heidi's hand and they made their way to the pastor's house, the congregation gazing after them. Some even followed to see if they went inside the pastor's house, which they did.

Then they gathered in little groups, talking about how strange it all was, keeping their eyes fixed on the pastor's door to see how the Alm Uncle would look when he came out.

Some, however, began saying the Alm Uncle wasn't so bad after all. "Did you see how gently he took the child's hand?" Others said they'd always thought people exaggerated how bad he was.

"Didn't I tell you?" said the baker. "Heidi wouldn't have come back from Frankfurt, where she was well fed and looked after, if he'd been cruel or unkind."

Soon, everybody was feeling quite friendly towards the Alm Uncle. The women remembered everything they'd been told by Peter and Grandmother and finally they all stood there, like people waiting for a long-lost friend.

Meanwhile, the Alm Uncle had gone into the pastor's house

and knocked at his study door. The pastor came out without looking surprised, for he had seen the Alm Uncle in church. He smiled and shook the Alm Uncle's hand so warmly the Alm Uncle couldn't speak at first. He had not expected such kindness. At last he said, "I've come to ask you to forget what I said when I last saw you. Forgive me for being so obstinate and for ignoring your advice. You were right, and I was wrong. I've decided to stay in Dörfli this winter. Heidi isn't strong enough to stand the bitter cold up on the mountain. And if the people here refuse to talk to me, it's no more than I deserve. And I know you won't do so."

The pastor's eyes shone with pleasure. "I'm so happy," he said, pressing the Alm Uncle's hand in his. "You won't regret coming to live here again. And you will always be welcome in my home as a dear friend. I look forward to us spending many winter evenings together. And we'll find friends for Heidi, too," he added, patting her head.

He walked with them both to the door, but didn't say goodbye until they were standing outside, so that all the people could see them shaking hands like the true friends they were.

The door had hardly shut before the whole congregation came forward to greet the Alm Uncle, everyone trying to be the first to shake his hand. There were so many hands held out to him, he didn't know where to begin. "We're so pleased to have you among us," someone said. "I've been wishing we could talk again," said another. And when the Alm Uncle said he was thinking of coming

When the Alm Uncle and Heidi were at last alone again, Heidi saw a look in his eyes she had never seen before.

back to Dörfli for the winter, there was such a chorus of delight that anyone would have thought he was the most beloved person in all of Dörfli.

As they left to go back up the mountain, many of the people went part of the way with them, begging them to come and visit before waving goodbye.

When the Alm Uncle and Heidi were at last alone again, Heidi saw a look in his eyes she had never seen before. "Grandfather, you look more and more beautiful today," she said. "Quite different from before."

"Do you think so?" he said with a smile. "I'm happier today than I had thought possible. It's good to be at peace with God and man. God was good to me when he brought you to my home."

When they reached Peter's house, Grandfather walked straight in. "Good morning," he said. "I think we'll have to do some more patching up before the winter winds come."

"Alm Uncle!" Grandmother exclaimed in surprise. "Now I can thank you for everything you've done for me." She stretched out her hand to him and Grandfather shook it warmly. "I have something in my heart to say to you," she went on. "If I have ever upset you, don't punish me by sending Heidi away again while I'm still alive. You don't know what that child means to me!" And she clasped Heidi to her.

"Don't worry, Grandmother," said the Alm Uncle. "I won't punish either of us by sending her away. We are together again and please God it will stay that way for many years to come."

Brigitte then drew the Alm Uncle to one side and showed him the hat with the feathers. "Heidi has given it to me," she said. "But of course I can't keep it."

"The hat is Heidi's," said Grandfather. "And if she doesn't wish to wear it any more, that's her choice. So do take it."

Brigitte was delighted. "It's worth more than ten pennies," she said, holding it up admiringly. "What wonderful things Heidi has brought back from Frankfurt. I have been wondering if I should send Peter there for a little while. Do you think it would do him good?"

Grandfather's eyes twinkled merrily. "It wouldn't do him any harm," he said. "But he had better wait for a good opportunity to come up first."

At that moment, Peter himself rushed in, knocking his head against the door in his haste. Breathless, he held out a letter in his hand. "It's for Heidi," he said. "It was delivered to the post office in Dörfli."

Everyone gasped, for no one in the house had ever received a letter before. Heidi sat down and opened it and they all gathered round to hear what was in it. The letter was from Clara.

"Everything's been so dull since you left," she wrote, "I haven't known how to bear it. But at last I've persuaded Father to take me to the baths at Ragaz this September, and Grandmamma has arranged to join us there. And after that, she says we can come and visit you and Grandfather. I'm so looking forward to it. Oh! And Grandmamma says that you were quite right to take the rolls. She is sending some coffee so Grandmother can have it with them, and she hopes to meet Grandmother herself when she comes to visit."

Everyone was so interested in Clara's news and talked about it for so long, that no one noticed the time passing, not even Grandfather.

"It's so lovely to see an old friend again," said Grandmother. "You will come again, Uncle, won't you? And you Heidi. Say you'll come tomorrow?"

Heidi and Grandfather promised to do so, and the two went back up the mountain. This time, the air was filled with the peal of church bells, growing fainter and fainter as they climbed. And there was the hut waiting for them, bathed in the light of the evening sun.

Chapter Fifteen

Preparations for a Journey

The friendly doctor who had given the order for Heidi to be sent home was walking up the broad street to Mr. Sesemann's house. It was a sunny September morning, so light and lovely you'd think it would make everybody happy. But the doctor was staring down at the white stones beneath his feet so he didn't notice the blue sky above. There was a sadness in his face that had never been there before, and his hair was now streaked with white.

The doctor had had just one daughter, who he'd been very close to since his wife's death and who had been his pride and joy. A few months ago, death had snatched the blooming girl from his side. He hadn't been the same man since.

Sebastian answered the door with the utmost courtesy and

leaped to serve him. Not only was the doctor a close friend of Mr. Sesemann and his daughter, but being so amiable, he had made friends of the whole household, as he did everywhere he went.

"Everything in order, Sebastian?" he asked amiably as he went upstairs. Sebastian followed, fussing devotedly, which went entirely unnoticed by the doctor, who had his back to him.

"I'm glad you've come," Mr. Sesemann cried as he entered the room. "We really must talk about the trip to Switzerland again. I need to know – do you absolutely stand by your view, even now that Clara's health has definitely improved?"

"My dear Sesemann, what am I going to do with you?" replied the doctor, sitting down with his friend. "I really wish your mother was here. With her, everything is simple and straightforward and stays on track. With you, there's just no sticking to a decision! This is the third time today you've had me here, only for me to tell you exactly the same thing each time."

"You're right. You must be losing patience with me. But you have to understand, my friend..." Mr. Sesemann laid his hand almost pleadingly on his friend's shoulder, "...it's just too difficult for me to deny the child something I promised her and she's looked forward to for months. She bore this last terrible phase so patiently, only in the hope that it was nearly time for the trip and that she would be able to visit her friend Heidi in the Alps. Now I must tell this good little girl, who already has so much to bear, that she cannot go. I just can't do it."

"You must," the doctor insisted. "Think it through. Clara hasn't had as bad a summer as this in years. There can be no question of such a long journey without serious consequences. What's more, the weather can be lovely on the Alps at this time of year, but it can turn very cold. Clara won't be able to spend the nights up on the mountain and the days are getting shorter, so she'd only be able visit Heidi for a couple of hours each day. The journey from Ragaz to the top will take hours, as Clara has to be carried there in a chair. In short, Sesemann, it's impossible."

His friend sat there silent and downcast. After a moment, the doctor added: "But look, I'll come with you to talk to Clara. She's a sensible girl. I'll tell her my plan. In May she can be taken to Ragaz. There, she can take a spa cure, and wait while the weather gets warmer on the Alps. Then she can be carried up from time to time. When she's refreshed and stronger, she'll enjoy it much more than she would be able to now. You must understand, Sesemann, if we are to hold out the least hope for your child's recovery, we must handle the situation with the utmost care."

Mr. Sesemann had listened with sad resignation up until this point, but now asked imploringly, "Doctor, do you hold out any hope for her recovery?"

The doctor shrugged, then said quietly, "Very little." After a moment, he went on, "But think of me, my dear friend. At least you still have a lovely little girl who misses you when you're away and is happy when you come home. You never have to come home to a gloomy house and sit at your table alone. And your child has a good life. She has a lot to put up with, certainly, but she also has a lot to enjoy. No, Sesemann, you don't have much to complain about. You've got each other for company, and that's a lot from where I'm sitting."

Mr. Sesemann had risen from his chair and was striding up and down the room as was his custom when deep in thought. Suddenly he stopped by his friend and clapped him on the shoulder. "I've had a thought. I can't bear to see you like this. You're not the same old fellow. You need something to take you out of yourself. You know what that something is? You have to take this trip yourself! You must visit Heidi in the Alps on our behalf."

The suggestion took the doctor by surprise and he wanted to protest, but Mr. Sesemann didn't give him a chance. He was so full of his new idea, that he grabbed his friend's arm and dragged him into his daughter's room.

Clara always loved visits from the doctor, who treated her so kindly and told her something funny or cheering every time he came. She knew why he was unable to do that now, and longed to be able to make him happy again. She reached out her hand to him and he sat down beside her. Mr. Sesemann pulled up a chair too and, putting his arm around his daughter, started to talk about the trip to Switzerland and how much he had been looking forward to it himself. He quickly skimmed over the main point of the matter – that they were now unable to go – as he feared tears. Then

he quickly passed onto the new idea, drawing Clara's attention to how much good it would do their friend to take the trip on their behalf.

Indeed, tears had appeared. Clara's blue eyes swam with them, despite her best efforts to stop them, for she knew how Papa hated to see her cry. But it was terribly hard that the trip to see Heidi was not to be, when it had been the only thing she had to look forward to through the whole, lonely summer. But Clara wasn't about to complain. She knew Papa would only forbid the trip if it would be bad for her. So she swallowed her tears and turned to the one hope left. She took her good friend's hand and implored him, "Do say that you'll go, dear Doctor. Visit Heidi and come right back to me and tell me what it's like up there, and what Heidi and Grandfather and Peter and the goats are all up to. I know them all so well! And then you can take the things I want to give Heidi. I've planned it all out. And something for Grandmother too. Please go, doctor. I'll take as much cod-liver oil as you want me to, while you're away."

Whether this decided the matter or not, is difficult to say, but one must suppose so, for the doctor smiled and said, "Then I must go, little Clara, and you will be hale and hearty again, as we want you to be, your Papa and I. When am I off? Have you decided that too?"

"It's best if you go first thing tomorrow morning," Clara replied.

"She's right," added her father. "The sun is shining, the sky is blue. There's no time to lose. Every day that goes by is a wasted one that you could have spent in the Alps."

The doctor laughed. "Next you'll be telling me off for still being here, Sesemann. I'd better be off."

He stood up but Clara clung to him. First she had to explain all the things she wanted him to take to Heidi, and tell him the messages that were to go along with each of them. She would send the package itself over to him later, as Miss Rottenmeyer had to help wrap it all up first. She was on one of her outings in town that always took a long time.

The doctor promised to deliver the package and all the messages safely. He promised to set out some time the following day if not first thing in the morning, and that on his return, he would tell Clara every single thing he'd seen and heard.

Servants of a household often have the strange gift of knowing things that are going on in the house long before their masters tell them anything about it. Sebastian and Tinette must have had this gift in excess, for just as Sebastian accompanied the doctor down the stairs, Tinette entered Clara's room, having only just been rung for.

"Fill this box with very fresh, soft cakes, like those we have with coffee, Tinette," said Clara, pointing to the cardboard box she had waiting. Tinette picked the box up by one corner contemptuously and let it dangle from her hand. At the door she said pertly, "It's hardly worth the effort."

As Sebastian opened the door with his usual courtesy, he said with a bow, "If the doctor would be so good, please tell the Little Miss that Sebastian says hello."

"Ah, Sebastian!" the doctor said amiably. "So you already know that I'm going away?"

Sebastian coughed a little. "Er - I - I - I can't remember how. Ah yes, I remember now: I happened to be going through the dining room when I heard the Little Miss's name being spoken, and so, you know how it is, I put two and two together..."

"Very well, very well," the doctor laughed. "Goodbye Sebastian. I'll pass on your message."

The doctor wanted to hurry out of the front door at this point but met with an obstacle. Miss Rottenmeyer had been prevented from continuing her walk by the strong wind, and so she had returned and was just about to come in through the open door. The large shawl which she was wrapped up in billowed out in the wind, so she looked very much like a ship in full sail. The doctor drew back for a moment. But Miss Rottenmeyer had a very special respect and regard for this man. She drew back with extreme politeness and for a while they both stood back considerately each making room for the other. Then at once, there was a gust of wind and Miss Rottenmeyer flew, full sails and all, right into the doctor. She had to take quite a few steps back to be able to greet the household friend in a more proper manner. Her forceful entrance had rather put her out, but the doctor had a way of soothing and smoothing ruffled feathers. He shared the news of his trip with her, and asked her in the nicest possible manner whether she could pack up the things that were to be sent to Heidi, in the way only she knew how. Then he took his leave.

Clara had expected a struggle before Miss Rottenmeyer would agree to pack up all the things she had chosen for Heidi. But this time she was mistaken: Miss Rottenmeyer was in an exceptionally good mood. She cleared everything off the big table to spread out the things Clara had gathered and to wrap them up right before her eyes. It was no easy task, for the things that were to be wrapped were all different shapes. First there was the thick cloak with the hood, that Clara had designed for Heidi, so that in the winter Heidi would be able to visit Grandmother without having to wait for Grandfather to come and fetch her with the blanket. Then there was the thick warm shawl for Grandmother, so she wouldn't feel the cold. Next was the big box of cakes. These were also meant for Grandmother so she'd have something other than bread rolls to eat with her coffee once in a while. Then there was a giant sausage. Originally Clara had meant this for Peter, who only ever had bread and cheese to eat. But then she had decided otherwise, as she was afraid Peter would be so excited he'd eat it all up at once. So now it was to be given to Brigitte, who could take a decent portion for herself and Grandmother before giving Peter his in stages. Next there was a little pouch of tobacco. That was for Grandfather, who liked to smoke a pipe when he sat in front of the hut in the evenings. Last of all came numerous mysterious little bags, boxes and packages which Clara had loved collecting, full of all kinds of surprises for Heidi to enjoy. Finally the work was finished and the great bundle lay on the floor ready for its journey.

Miss Rottenmeyer looked at it, sunk deep in thoughts of the art of packing. Clara looked at it happily and expectantly, imagining Heidi, and how she would leap in the air and cry out in surprise when the giant package arrived. Then Sebastian came in and swung the giant package onto his shoulder, and took it without delay to the doctor's house.

Chapter Sixteen

A guest on the Alm

Dawn glowed red over the mountains, and a fresh morning wind rushed through the pines and blew the old branches to and fro. Heidi's eyes sprang open. The noise had awoken her. The sound of the wind in the pines always touched Heidi's innermost being and drew her outside to stand beneath the trees. She leaped from her bed, hardly stopping to get dressed. She hopped down the little ladder – Grandfather's bed was already empty – and sprang out of the door. Grandfather was standing just outside and looking up at the sky and all around, as he did every morning to see how the day was going to turn out.

Small, rosy clouds were drifting overhead, and the sky grew bluer and bluer. Gold came flowing over the far mountains and pastures, as the sun rose over the clifftops.

"Oh, how beautiful! Good morning, Grandfather," Heidi called as she bounded up to him.

"Bright-eyed and bushy-tailed?" laughed Grandfather.

Heidi ran over to the pines and jumped for joy under the waving branches. At each new gust of wind, she cried out and jumped a little higher.

In the meantime, Grandfather had gone into the stalls and milked Little Swan and Little Bear. He had already washed and brushed them ready for their trip up the mountain, and he led them out from the stalls. As soon as Heidi saw her friends, she bounced over and flung her arms around their necks. She greeted them tenderly and they bleated happily and trustingly. Each goat wanted to show Heidi more affection and pushed its head harder and harder against her shoulder until she was squashed between the two of them. But she wasn't afraid, and when the lively Little Bear pushed too hard, she just said, "No, Little Bear, now you're pushing like big Bullfinch," and the goat pulled his head back right away and stood there quietly. Little Swan had already pulled her head back, and had an expression on her face that seemed to say, 'Nobody could accuse me of acting like Bullfinch.' Little Swan was better behaved than Little Bear.

From below came Peter's whistle, and in the next moment all the lively goats came leaping up, with nimble Goldfinch springing away in front. At once Heidi was in the middle of the herd, and was pushed here and there amid all the noisy greetings from her friends. She pushed through to say hello to shy little Snowflake who was trying to reach Heidi but was being pushed away by the bigger ones.

Peter appeared behind them, and did a last, low whistle to shoo the goats away onto the pasture, so he had space to speak to Heidi.

"Can you come with me today?" he said rather abruptly.

"I can't, Peter," answered Heidi. "I must be here when my visitors come from Frankfurt."

"Uncle would be here anyway," grumbled Peter.

Grandfather's voice boomed from the hut, "Why is the army being held up? Is there a problem with the Field Marshall or with the troops?"

At once, Peter did an about-turn, swinging his stick in the air until it hummed. The goats who knew the noise well, fled before it, and Peter trotted after them up the mountain.

Ever since Heidi had come home to her Grandfather's, she thought of doing things that would never have entered her head before. Every morning she made her bed very carefully, stroking it until it was smooth. Then she ran about the hut, putting chairs in their right places, and putting everything that was lying around away in the cupboard. Then she got a cloth, climbed onto a stool and rubbed the table until it was spotless. When Grandfather came back in, he looked around approvingly and said, "Every day is

Sunday at our house. Heidi didn't go away for nothing."

Today, after Peter had made himself scarce and she had eaten breakfast with Grandfather, she busied herself again, but nearly couldn't finish. It was such a beautiful day outside, and every moment something would interrupt her work. A sunbeam shot in through the open window so lovely and bright, as if it was calling to her, "Come out, Heidi! Come out!" She couldn't stay in the hut any longer, and ran outside. The sparkling sunshine lit up the hut, and everything around it, from the mountains to the valley far below. The cliffs looked so golden and summery, she had to sit down for a moment to look at them. Then she remembered the three stools still standing in the middle of the floor and all the breakfast things still lying on the table. She leaped to her feet and ran back inside. But before long, the wind started rushing through the pines so much that Heidi felt it in all her limbs. She had to go back outside and dance beneath the swaying branches.

Meanwhile, Grandfather had all kinds of jobs to do in the workshop behind the hut. He came to the door from time to time to watch Heidi's antics with a smile on his face. He'd just gone back inside, when Heidi yelled out, "Grandfather! Come quickly!"

He rushed out, fearing there might be something wrong. But then he saw her running towards the slope shouting, "They're coming! They're coming! And the doctor's at the front!"

Heidi rushed towards her old friend. He stretched out his hand to her, and she hugged his whole outstretched arm and burst out joyfully, "Good morning, Doctor. And thank you a million times over."

"Hello there Heidi. What are you thanking me for?" the doctor asked with a friendly smile.

"For letting me come home to Grandfather," the little girl explained.

The doctor's face lit up. He hadn't expected such a welcome. He had climbed the mountain lost in thoughts about his loneliness and hadn't even seen how beautiful it was all around him. He assumed that little Heidi would hardly recognize him as he'd seen so little of her, and he thought of himself as only the bearer of bad news, who nobody really likes to welcome. Instead of all this, Heidi's eyes shone with sheer happiness, and she still held tightly onto her good friend's arm, full of love and gratitude.

With a fatherly tenderness, he took the child's arm. "Come on, Heidi," he said warmly, "lead me to your Grandfather and show me your home."

But Heidi stayed put and gazed down the mountain wonderingly. "Where are Clara and Grandmamma?" she asked.

"Now I have to tell you something that will upset you, and it pains me too," replied the doctor. "You see, Heidi, I've come on my own. Clara was too ill to travel, and so Grandmamma hasn't come either. But in the spring, when the days grow warm and long again, they will definitely come."

Heidi stood there silently, stunned by the news. For a moment she couldn't grasp that everything she imagined so clearly would not happen in reality. The doctor stood quietly in front of her, and all around them was silence, apart from the wind rushing through the pines above. Then Heidi suddenly remembered why she had run down in the first place, and that the doctor himself had come and was there. She looked up at him. There was something so sad in the eyes that looked back at her. It hadn't been there when the doctor had looked at her in Frankfurt. It cut Heidi to the quick for she couldn't bear to see anyone sad, least of all the good doctor. He must be sad because Clara and Grandmamma couldn't come. She quickly tried to think of a way to comfort him.

"Oh, it won't be long until spring," she said comfortingly. "And then Clara will be able to stay for longer, which will be much better. Let's go up to Grandfather." Hand in hand with her friend, she climbed up to the hut. Heidi was thinking so hard about how to make the good doctor happy again, that she even began to believe it herself. It would really be such a short time until spring on the Alm, that one would hardly notice the wait. She was so convinced by her own words of comfort, that she called out very cheerfully up to Grandfather, "They're not here, but it won't be long before they come too."

The doctor was no stranger to Grandfather, as Clara had told him so much about him. The old man held out his hand to his guest and said, "Welcome." Then the two men sat down on the bench outside the hut. They made room for Heidi too, and the doctor waved her over to sit by him. Then he started to tell how Mr. Sesemann had encouraged him to take the trip, saying how good it would be for him.

"And indeed it was," the doctor added. "I've not felt this well for a long time. And something else will soon be coming up the mountain," he whispered in Heidi's ear. "Something that has come all the way from Frankfurt with me that will bring you more pleasure than the arrival of an old doctor." Heidi couldn't wait to see what it could be.

Grandfather tried to encourage the doctor to spend the lovely September days on the Alm, or at least to come up on every sunny day. "I've no bed to offer you, but don't go all the way back to Ragaz," Grandfather advised. "Take a room down in Dörfli. You'll be able to find a room in the inn there – simple, but clean and tidy. Then you could come up the mountain every morning, which would do you the power of good. And I'd gladly show you any parts of the mountains you would like to see."

The doctor liked this plan very much, and they decided to put it into action.

By now, the sun had reached midday. The wind had long since dropped and the pines had grown still. The air was, for the altitude, still mild and lovely and a refreshing breeze reached the sunny bench.

The Alm Uncle stood up and went inside the hut. He came back with a table which he set before the bench. "So Heidi, can you bring what we need for lunch?" he said. "The gentleman must excuse us – our kitchen is simple, but the dining room is excellent."

"I agree," replied the doctor, gazing down at the sunlit valley. "I'd be delighted to accept. I'm sure everything tastes delicious up here."

Heidi ran back and forth, busy as a squirrel, and brought everything that she could find in the cupboard. Having the chance to wait on the doctor made her enormously happy. Grandfather prepared the food and came out with a steaming jug of milk and the gleaming, golden toasted cheese. Then he cut some fine slices of the meat that he had dried in the pure mountain air. The doctor found his lunch more delicious than anything he had eaten all year.

"Yes, yes, Clara must certainly come here," he said. "She'll gain new strength if she eats for a while as I have today. She'll get sturdier and stronger than she's ever been in her life."

Just then, someone came up the mountain, with a huge bundle on his back. As he arrived at the hut, he threw his burden down on the ground and took a couple of deep lungfuls of the fresh mountain air.

"Ah, here it is – the thing that came from Frankfurt with me," said the doctor getting to his feet and pulling Heidi with him. They went to the bundle and started to undo it. When the first heavy cover was undone, he said, "There you go, little one, now you can undo the rest yourself and discover the treasure."

Heidi did just that and cried out with big, round eyes at everything she unpacked. "Look at what there is for Grandmother," said the doctor, pointing to the big, cardboard box.

"Oh! Oh! Now Grandmother has lovely cakes to eat for once!" Heidi cried, leaping around the box. She was about to take it to Grandmother right away, but Grandfather stopped her. "We'll go down this evening, with the doctor, and take it then," he told her. So Heidi went back to the bundle. She found the lovely pouch of tobacco and brought it over to Grandfather. He was very pleased. He filled his pipe with it and chatted with the doctor about all kinds of things, sitting on the bench and puffing out great clouds of smoke, while Heidi leaped here and there between her treasures.

Eventually she came back to the bench, stood by the doctor and at the first pause in their conversation, said very firmly: "No, it didn't bring me more pleasure than the arrival of an old doctor."

Both men chuckled. "Well I hadn't expected that," said the doctor, beaming with pleasure.

When the sun was half sunk behind the mountains, their guest stood up to begin his return journey to Dörfli and to book his room there. Grandfather tucked the big sausage and the shawl into the same box as the cakes, then picked up the box in his arms. The doctor took Heidi's hand and they all strolled down the mountain to Goat Peter's hut. Here Heidi said goodbye. She was to wait inside with Grandmother until Grandfather picked her up again, as he had decided to accompany their guest down to Dörfli. When the doctor took Heidi's hand to say goodbye, she asked him, "Would you like to go up to the pasture with the goats tomorrow? I think it's the best thing to do in the whole world."

"Agreed," said the doctor. "We'll go together."

So the men went on. Grandfather had left the big cardboard box by the front door and Heidi heaved it inside to show Grandmother. She brought everything as close to Grandmother as possible, so that she could feel it all and know what it was. The shawl she draped around Grandmother's shoulders.

"It's all from Frankfurt, from Clara and Grandmamma," she said to the astonished old lady and to Brigitte, who was rooted to the spot with surprise.

"You must be so pleased with the cakes, Grandmother. See how soft they are," Heidi said, and Grandmother assured her, "Of course I am, Heidi. What good people they are!" Then she stroked the soft, warm shawl again and said, "But this is something really wonderful for the cold winter. It's so luxurious. I never thought I'd have something like this in my whole life."

Heidi was very surprised that Grandmother could be more pleased with the shawl than the cakes. Brigitte was still sitting in the same spot, staring at the sausage which lay on the table. She'd never seen such an enormous sausage in all her life and she couldn't quite believe that this one was hers, to cut up herself. She shook her head and said shyly, "I'll have to ask the Alm Uncle what this is meant for."

She brought everything as close to Grandmother as possible, so that she could feel it all and know what it was.

"To eat, of course. Nothing else," Heidi said without hesitation.

Just then, Peter came stumbling in. "The Alm Uncle's behind me. He said Heidi should–" but he stopped there. He was looking at the table, where the sausage lay, and was so overpowered by the sight of it that he couldn't say another word. But Heidi knew what he had meant, and said goodbye to Grandmother.

Now, whenever the Alm Uncle passed by the hut, he would pop in to say hello to Grandmother. She always perked up when she heard his footsteps too, as he always had a cheery word for her. But today it was late for Heidi, who had been out in the sunshine all day. Grandfather stayed outside and called in through the open door, "The child must get some sleep. Good night!" When Heidi bounced outside to him, he took her hand. Under the glimmering starlit skies, the two strolled home to their peaceful hut on the mountain.

Chapter Seventeen

A compensation

Early the next morning, the doctor climbed up the mountain from Dörfli with Peter and his goats. He tried to start a conversation with the boy, but only received a couple of monosyllabic answers. Peter wasn't easily drawn into conversation. So the group wandered in silence up to the Alm hut, where Heidi was already waiting with both of her goats, all three as bright and cheerful as the early sunshine on the peaks.

"You coming?" asked Peter, as he did every morning.

"Of course, if the doctor's coming," Heidi replied.

Peter looked sideways at the doctor.

Then Grandfather joined them with a lunch bag in his hand. First he said good morning to them all, then he went to Peter and hung the bag over his shoulder.

It was heavier than usual, for the Alm Uncle had packed a good hunk of the dried meat in it too. He thought the doctor might like to eat lunch with the children up on the meadow. Peter grinned from ear to ear, as he guessed that something unusual was hidden in the bag.

They started off up the mountain. Heidi was surrounded by goats, all pushing and shoving one another out of the way to walk next to her. She went a little way being jostled along, but soon stopped to tell them off. "Run along properly now, and don't keep coming pushing and shoving me. I'm going to walk with the doctor." Then she patted Snowflake gently on the back and warned her in particular to be good. Working her way out of the herd, she went over to the doctor, who took her hand.

He didn't need to make any great effort to start a conversation as he had with Peter. Heidi began chatting right away, telling him all about the different goats and their strange little ways, and about the flowers up on the meadow and the cliffs and birds. He didn't notice the time flying by and before he knew it, they were up on the meadow. Peter had been casting dark, sideways glances at the doctor all the way up the mountain, which could have given him quite a fright, but luckily he didn't notice.

At the top of the mountain, Heidi took her good friend straight to the most beautiful spot, where she always went to look at the view. She sat down on the sunny grass and the doctor sat

At the top of the mountain, Heidi took her good friend straight to the most beautiful spot... where she always went to to look at the view.

down next to her. The golden autumnal day lit up the peaks and the wide, green valley. And all around, tinkling goat bells could be heard, so sweet and uplifting, as if they were ringing out to mark some joyous occasion.

Opposite them, golden sunbeams glittered and sparkled on the snow-covered mountain, and Falknis lifted its towering cliffs majestically high into the dark blue sky. The morning wind blew quietly and blissfully over the Alm, gently moving the last of the summer harebells, which waved their heads in the warm sunshine. Overhead, the big eagle was circling in the sky, but today he remained silent. With outstretched wings, he swam calmly through the blue.

Heidi looked all around. The cheerfully nodding flowers, the blue sky, the merry sunshine, the contented bird in the sky, everything was just so beautiful. Her eyes sparkled with joy. Then she looked to see if her friend was enjoying it too, and could see how beautiful everything was. Until now, the doctor had been quietly and thoughtfully looking all around. As he met the child's shining eyes, he said, "Yes Heidi, it's beautiful here. But what do you think? If someone brought a sad heart here, how could they make it better so they could enjoy all this beauty?"

"Oh," Heidi cried happily, "you can't be sad here, only in Frankfurt."

The doctor smiled a little but the smile soon faded. "And if someone came and brought all the sadness from Frankfurt with them, Heidi," he said. "Do you know what could help him then?"

"You just have to tell God, if you don't know what else to do," Heidi said confidently.

"That's a good idea, child," the doctor remarked. "But what if the reason he's so miserable is something that can't be changed. Then what is there to tell God?"

Heidi had to think about this for a moment. But she was entirely certain that help could be gained from God for every kind of misery. She tried to answer from her own experience. After a moment she said with confidence, "Then you have to wait. And you have to keep thinking: now God must know of something happy that will come after this thing. Even if you can't see it just then for your misery. Then suddenly you'll see very clearly the good thing that God had in mind."

"That's a wonderful thought. You must hang on to that, Heidi," said the doctor. For a while, he looked silently down at the mighty clifftops and across the green, sunlit valley, and then said, "You see, Heidi, someone could sit here, with a great big shadow over his eyes, so that he wasn't able to appreciate the beauty that lies all around him. Then his heart would grow doubly sad, where it could have felt so happy. Can you understand that?"

At that, Heidi felt a bolt of pain in her happy heart. The great big shadow over the eyes reminded her of Grandmother, who could no longer see the bright sunshine and the beauty up here. It caused sorrow in Heidi's heart which arose afresh every time she remembered it. She was quiet a moment, for the pain had stunned her. Then she said solemnly, "Yes, I can understand that. But I have an idea: then you have to say Grandmother's hymns. They make everything a bit lighter and sometimes so light that you even get happy again. That's what Grandmother said."

"Which hymns, Heidi?" asked the doctor.

"I only know the one with the sun and the garden and the other long one that Grandmother likes so much she makes me read it three times," replied Heidi.

"Tell me them. I'd like to hear them too," and the doctor settled himself to listen.

Heidi folded her hands together, and gathered her thoughts. "Should I start at the part where Grandmother says her heart fills with faith again?"

The doctor nodded.

So Heidi began:

Leave the plans to him, for He
is wiser than you guess.
You'll wonder at the way He makes
things turn out for the best.

Sometimes it may seem
that He has disappeared,
that He's abandoned you

in your very hour of need.

But if you only keep your faith
then it will come to pass,
He'll release you from your sorrow
and raise you up at last.

Heidi stopped suddenly. She wasn't sure whether the doctor was still listening. He had put his hand over his eyes and was sitting very still. She thought he'd dropped off, and if he woke up and wanted to hear more verses, then she could say them. All was quiet. The doctor didn't say a word, but he wasn't asleep. The words had taken him back to days gone by. He was a little boy again, standing next to his beloved mother's armchair. She had her arm around his neck and was reciting the hymn to him as Heidi read it out. He hadn't heard it in a long time. Now he heard his mother's voice again and saw her good eyes resting on him so lovingly, and as the words of the verse had ended, he had heard her lovely voice saying other things to him besides. He must have been happy listening to it, as he sat there for a long time, with his hand over his face, silent and motionless. When he finally looked up, he saw Heidi gazing curiously at him. He took the little girl's hand in his.

"Heidi your hymn was beautiful," he said, and his voice sounded happier than it had before. "We will come back here another time, and you can recite it to me again."

From the moment they'd arrived on the pasture, Peter had been busy venting his anger. Heidi hadn't been up to the meadow with him in days and now that she was finally there, that old man was sitting by her the whole time, and Peter couldn't get close to her. He was furious about it. He took up a position some distance behind the unsuspecting doctor, so that he couldn't see him, and first waved one fist around in the air threateningly, and after a while both fists. The longer Heidi stayed sitting by the doctor, the harder Peter clenched his fists and the higher and more menacingly he waved them behind the man's back.

Meanwhile the sun had reached the point in the sky that meant midday and lunchtime. Peter recognized it well. Suddenly he screamed with all his might, "Time to eat!"

Heidi stood up and wanted to fetch the sack, so that the doctor could stay where he was to eat his lunch. But he said he wasn't hungry, that all he wanted was a glass of milk to drink, and then he'd like to wander around on the mountain and climb a little further.

Heidi found that she wasn't hungry either, and only wanted to drink some milk, and after that she would lead the doctor up to the big, moss-covered rocks high up where Goldfinch once nearly jumped down and where all the most fragrant plants grew. She ran over to Peter and explained everything to him and said he had to get a bowl of milk from Little Swan for the doctor, and then another for her. Peter stared at Heidi in astonishment and asked, "Who will eat what's in the sack?"

"You can have it, but you have to get the milk first," Heidi answered.

Peter did as he was told. He'd never done anything as quickly before because he was thinking all the time about the sack and wondering what was inside that was now his, and his alone. As soon as the other two were quietly drinking their milk, Peter opened the sack and peered inside. When he saw the wonderful piece of meat, his whole body shook with delight. He had to look in again to make sure it was true.

He put his hand into the sack to take the treasure out and enjoy it. But suddenly he drew his hand back, as if he'd been burned. He had just remembered how he'd stood behind the doctor and waved his fists at him. This very same man was now giving him his entire lunch. Peter now regretted waving his fists, as it seemed somehow to be preventing him from being able to enjoy the lovely food.

He sprang to his feet and ran over to the spot where he had stood waving his fists. Then he stretched both hands out flat in the air, to show that the fists didn't count any more. He stayed like that for quite a while, until he had the feeling that he'd balanced things out again. Then he came bounding back to the sack and, now that his conscience was clear, started to enjoy his unusually delicious lunch.

The doctor and Heidi had wandered around with one another chatting amiably. But now the gentleman decided it was time to go back. He said Heidi should stay with her goats but Heidi wouldn't hear of the doctor going down the mountain all alone. She said she would accompany him to Grandfather's hut and maybe a little further.

So the two said goodbye to Peter, and went hand in hand back down the mountain. They talked about all kinds of things on the way. Heidi showed him all the places where the goats liked to graze and where yellow willowherb and red centaury grew, and other flowers too. She knew all their names, for throughout the summer Grandfather had taught her all the ones he knew.

When they were a little way past Grandfather's hut, the doctor told Heidi to turn back and go home. So they said goodbye to one another, and the doctor went down the mountain. Every now and then he turned back, and saw Heidi, still standing waving to him, just like his own dear daughter used to do whenever he left the house.

It was a clear, sunny September. Every morning, the doctor came up to the Alm and then went on a beautiful walk. Often the Alm Uncle would go with him, high into the clifftops, where the old, weathered pines nodded over them. The eagle must have lived nearby for he came swooping right over their heads, shrieking at them. The doctor enjoyed the Alm Uncle's conversation, and was in awe of his knowledge of the mountains. He knew all the alpine plants that grew there and what they were good for, from the hearty pines and dark fir trees with their fragrant needles, to the curled moss that sprang up between old tree roots, and all the delicate, little plants and tiny, hidden flowers that spring to life on the high alpine ground.

The old man knew all about the animals, both big and small, who lived up there between the rocks, in burrows and in the treetops, and he told the doctor some funny stories about them.

Time flew by for the doctor on these outings and often, when he shook the Uncle's hand to say goodbye at the end of the day, he found himself saying yet again, "Good friend, I never leave you without having learned something new."

But on many of the days he spent on the mountain, usually the most beautiful, he would go out with Heidi. Then the two would sit together on the spot they had shared on the first day, and Heidi would recite a hymn for the doctor and then tell him whatever she knew. Peter would sit a little way from them, but he was quite calm now and didn't wave his fists any more.

Eventually the fine September month came to an end. One morning, the doctor arrived not looking as happy as usual. He said it was his last day. He had to go back to Frankfurt. He was sorry to leave, for he'd come to love the mountain as if it were his home. The Alm Uncle was sorry to hear the news, for he had enjoyed talking to the doctor, and Heidi was so used to seeing her lovely friend every day that she couldn't quite believe he was going. The doctor said goodbye to Grandfather and asked if Heidi could accompany him a little way. They went down the mountain holding hands in silence.

After a while the doctor stopped and said that Heidi had come far enough, and should turn back. He stroked the child's hair gently with his hand and said, "I have to go, Heidi. Oh, if only I could take you with me to Frankfurt and keep you."

Frankfurt rose up in Heidi's mind. The many, many houses and stone streets and Miss Rottenmeyer and Tinette... She answered timidly, "I'd rather you came to us again."

"Yes, it's better that way around. Take care, Heidi," he said warmly, and held his hand out. Heidi put her hand in his and looked up at him. The good eyes that were looking down at her were brimming with tears. The doctor turned quickly and hurried down the mountain.

Heidi didn't move. The doctor's tears had affected her deeply. Suddenly she burst into loud sobs and plunged down the slope after him, crying with all her might, "Doctor! Doctor!"

He stopped and turned around.

The little girl caught up with him, tears streaming down her cheeks. "I will come with you to Frankfurt right now and stay with you as long as you like. I just have to tell Grandfather first."

The doctor stroked her hair soothingly. "No, no, my dear Heidi," he said gently. "Not right now. You have to stay here with your pines, or you'll be ill again. But come, I want to ask you something: if I'm ever unwell and alone, would you come and stay with me? I would like to think that someone would love and take care of me then."

"Yes, yes, of course. I'd come on the very day you sent for me. I love you almost as much as Grandfather," said Heidi, still sobbing.

The doctor pressed her hand in his, then set off again quickly. Heidi stayed in the same spot and waved and waved, until the gentleman was only a tiny spot on the path ahead. As he turned for the last time and looked back at Heidi waving and the sunny Alp, he said quietly to himself, "It's good for a person, being up there. It can heal both body and soul, and one can learn to be happy again."

Chapter Eighteen

Winter in Dörfli

The snow was so deep on the Alm, that Goat Peter's hut looked as if the windows were at ground level, for nothing could be seen of the hut below them. The front door had disappeared completely. Every night it snowed more and more, and every morning Peter would leap out of the window and sink so deep into the soft snow that he would have to thrash about with all his limbs to work his way out. Then his mother would pass a broom out of the window, and Peter would poke and shove a path to the front door. There he'd have his work cut out to dig out the door.

This job always fell to Peter, as only he was small enough to slip out of the window. Otherwise as the snow melted and the door opened, the whole lot would fall into the kitchen. Or else it would freeze solid and they would all be walled in.

But the ice and snow brought its comforts, too. Whenever Peter had to go down to Dörfli, he simply opened the window and crawled out into the snow. Then his mother would push his toboggan out after him and he only had to sit on it to go in any direction he chose, for the entire mountain was one great toboggan run.

Uncle wasn't on the Alm in the wintertime. He had kept his promise. As soon as the first snow fell, he left his hut and stalls and moved with Heidi and the goats down to Dörfli. Near the church there was a tumbledown old ruin. It was clear that it had once been a grand house, even though most of the building had entirely collapsed.

The house had belonged to a high-ranking soldier, who had been in service in Spain. He had fought bravely there and acquired great riches. Then he'd come home to Dörfli and built this grand house to live in. But he didn't stay long. Having lived out in the noisy world, he found that quiet village life now bored him. So he moved back to the hustle and bustle, never to return.

Many years later, when the owner was presumed long-dead, a distant relative from the valley took over the house. It was already falling down by then and the new owner didn't want to rebuild it. So he rented it to poor people for very little money, and if more of the building fell down, it was left like that.

Then, when the Alm Uncle had come back to Dörfli with his

son, Tobias, he moved into the ruined house and lived there. Since then it had mostly been empty, for the winter in Dörfli was long and cold, and no one could live in that house unless they first patched up all the holes. The wind blew and whistled through the rooms from all sides, put out lights and made the inhabitants shiver. But the Alm Uncle knew how to look after himself. As soon as he'd decided to spend the winter in Dörfli, he'd taken on the old house again, and had come down throughout September to work on making it suitable to live in. In the middle of October, he moved down with Heidi.

Approaching the house from the back, you came to an open-air room, with just one crumbling wall. Over this there were the arched remains of a window, with thick ivy growing around them up to the crumbled ceiling. The remains of the ceiling were beautifully domed, as this room had once been the chapel.

Through an open doorway was a grand hall. It had decorative stone flags with grass growing between them. The walls and half the ceiling were gone, and the rest looked like it would fall on your head at any moment, were it not for the two thick columns holding it up. Grandfather had put wooden boards around it and strewn straw on the floor, for this is where the goats were to live.

After that there were all kinds of passageways, with gaps where the sky or the meadow or street were visible. Then came a heavy oak door that was firm and straight. Inside, was a big room that was still as solid as ever. The four firm walls had dark wooden panelling, and in the corner was a huge, tiled stove that reached almost to the ceiling. The tiles had big, blue pictures painted on them. One had an old tower surrounded by tall trees, with a hunter and his dogs walking beneath them. Another had a calm lake under oak trees, with a fisherman holding his rod out over the water. A low bench ran all the way around the whole stove, so Heidi ran and sat down on it to study the pictures. She loved this room. As she was shuffling along the bench something else caught her eye. Between the stove and the wall four boards had been nailed together. Inside them was her bed, exactly as it had been on the Alm: a big heap of hay with a linen sheet and a blanket for a cover. "Oh Grandfather, this is my room! How lovely!" Heidi cried out. "But where are you going to sleep?"

"Your bed is by the stove, so you don't

freeze," said Grandfather. "Mine is in here."

Grandfather opened a door, and Heidi hopped though into the next room behind him. Inside was a small room where he had built a bed for himself. There was yet another door in the room, which Heidi opened. Then she stood, silent with awe at the sight before her. It was the most gigantic kitchen she had ever seen in her life. It had been a lot of work for Grandfather, who had a lot more to do besides, for there were countless holes in the walls. He had already boarded up so many that it looked as if there were lots of wooden cupboards all around the walls.

He had also patched up the huge, ancient door with boards and nails so that it shut tight. It was a good job too, for outside there were fallen-down walls covered in thick undergrowth which was home to hordes of beetles and lizards.

Heidi liked their new house, and by the next day, when Peter came to see it, she had already examined every corner and crevice so she didn't let him rest until she had shown him every inch. It was a very thorough tour.

Heidi slept superbly in her corner by the stove, but in the morning she kept thinking she'd woken up on the mountain and wanted to open the door to see whether the pines were silent because there was snow weighing down their branches. It was a few moments before she remembered where she was, and each time she felt a weight on her heart when she saw she wasn't up on the mountain. But when she heard Grandfather talking to Little Swan and Little Bear and the goats bleated so loudly and merrily, as if to say, "Come on Heidi!" then she knew she was still at home, and jumped happily out of bed to race into their stall.

On the fourth day, however, Heidi said anxiously, "I have to go up to see Grandmother. I can't leave her alone for so long."

But Grandfather wouldn't allow it. "Not today nor tomorrow," he said. "The Alm has snow on it fathoms deep and it's still snowing. Even Peter can hardly get through it. A little one like you, Heidi, would be covered up on the spot and nobody would be able to find you. Wait a bit until it freezes, and then you can walk over the top of it."

Heidi didn't like the idea of waiting. But her days were so full she hardly noticed them passing. Every morning and afternoon, she went to school now in Dörfli and learned everything there was to learn with great enthusiasm. Peter was hardly ever seen there, for he hardly ever went. The teacher was a mild man, and only said every now and then, "It seems Peter isn't here again. School would do him good, but perhaps there's so much snow up there he can't get through."

In the late afternoon, however, when school had finished for the day, Peter usually did manage to get through so as to visit Heidi.

After some days, the sun came out again, casting its golden beams over the white ground. It dropped behind the mountains early, unwilling to gaze down into the valley for too long now the greenery and blooms of summer were gone. That evening, the moon rose, huge and luminous, lighting up the night over all the snow, and the following morning the mountain glittered and sparkled from top to bottom like crystal.

When Peter leaped out of the window as usual, he found a surprise. Instead of sinking into the snow, he slid partway down the mountain like a runaway ski. When he eventually got to his feet, he stamped with all his might, to make sure it was true. It was: however hard he stamped and dug with his heels, he couldn't splinter the ice. The entire Alm had frozen solid. It was as hard as stone.

Peter was glad, as he knew that this meant Heidi could visit. He scrambled back to his hut, and back in through the window, for the front door was walled shut by the ice. He gulped down the milk his mother had laid on the table, stuffed the piece of bread in his pocket and blurted, "I have to go to school."

"Yes, go and do your lessons, there's a good boy," said his mother.

Peter crawled out through the window, pulling his toboggan out after himself. Then he sat down on it and shot down the mountain. He went like lightning, tore straight through Dörfli, out the other side and halfway down to Mayenfeld. He didn't dare stop the toboggan for fear of doing himself or it an injury. So he carried on until he got to flat ground and it slowed to a stop by itself. Then he got off and looked back. "I'll be late for school anyway now," he thought as it was at least an hour's climb back up to the schoolhouse. So he took his time, and arrived back up at Dörfli just as Heidi had come home and sat down with Grandfather to eat lunch. Peter burst in and blurted: "It's happened."

"What? Who has it happened to?" said the Alm Uncle.

"The snow," said Peter.

"Oh! That means I can go up to see Grandmother!" Heidi rejoiced, understanding Peter's meaning perfectly. "But Peter, why weren't you at school? You could toboggan down really easily," she said reproachfully, for Heidi didn't think it was acceptable for him to stay away from school if he could get there.

"Went too far with the toboggan. Was too late," Peter replied.

"That's called desertion," said the Alm Uncle. "And people who do that have their ears pulled, do you hear me?"

Peter tugged his cap in fear, for he had more respect for the Alm Uncle than anyone else in the world.

"And a General like you should be doubly ashamed to be a deserter," the Alm Uncle continued. "If your goats all wandered here and there and refused to follow you and do what was good for them, what would you do?"

"Beat them," said Peter immediately.

"And if a boy did the same, and got beaten for it, what would you say?"

"Serve him right," said Peter.

"So now you know, Goat General. If you slide past school

on your toboggan again when you should be inside, come to me afterwards to get what you deserve."

Peter suddenly understood what he was talking about and that he was supposed to be the boy compared to the goats. He looked fearfully into the corners of the room to see if there was a stick lying around anywhere.

But the Alm Uncle said quite cheerfully, "Come and sit down at the table now, and have some lunch. Afterwards Heidi can go with you. If you bring her home again this evening you'll find some dinner here too."

This unexpected turn of events pleased Peter no end. He beamed from ear to ear and obediently sat down by Heidi right away. She was so excited about seeing Grandmother she couldn't eat another mouthful. She pushed her plate, which still had a big potato and grilled cheese on it, towards Peter. Grandfather had already filled a plate for him, so he had a mountain of food. He tackled it undaunted.

Heidi ran to the cupboard and got her cloak that Clara had sent her. She stood and waited, ready for the journey, wrapped up warm with her hood up. When Peter had shovelled in his last mouthful, she said, "Come on then!" and they set off.

Heidi had a lot to tell Peter. She began by telling him all about Little Swan and Little Bear, who hadn't eaten a thing in their new stall, and hung their heads and said nothing all day long.

"Grandfather says they're doing what I did in Frankfurt," she went on. "For they have never been down from the Alm in their lives before. If you only knew how awful that feels."

The pair had almost reached the top without Peter having said a single word. He had been deep in thought all the way and not really listening to Heidi at all. When they reached the hut, he said rather moodily, "I'll go to school then rather than get what the Alm Uncle said he'd give me."

"Quite right," agreed Heidi.

Inside, Peter's mother sat mending some old clothes, but Grandmother's chair by the spinning wheel was empty.

"Where is Grandmother?" asked Heidi.

"She's stayed in bed the past few days," explained Brigitte. "She said it was too cold for her to get up and besides, she hasn't been feeling very well."

This was a shock to Heidi. Usually Grandmother was to be found sitting in her place in the corner. She ran straight into the old lady's bedroom. There she lay, wrapped in her new shawl in her narrow bed, with the thin blanket on top.

"Thank the Lord," Grandmother said as soon as she heard Heidi bounding in. She had been unbearably anxious, as she always was when she didn't see Heidi for a while. Peter had told her that a stranger had come from Frankfurt, and had wanted to talk with Heidi when they were all up on the pasture. Grandmother had been worried the man had come to take Heidi away. Even after he had left, her fear continued, for he could easily send someone to pick the little girl up for him.

Heidi jumped onto the old lady's bed. "Are you terribly unwell, Grandmother?" she asked concernedly.

"No, no, child," said the old lady, stroking Heidi's hair lovingly. "It's just the cold has crept into my bones a little."

"Will you be better as soon as it gets warm again?" Heidi went on.

"Yes, God willing, so I can sit at my spinning wheel again. I wanted to try today. I'm sure I'll be able to tomorrow," Grandmother said, for she'd sensed that Heidi was scared.

Her words reassured Heidi, who had indeed been frightened by the sight of Grandmother kept to her bed. She looked at her curiously for a moment and then said, "In Frankfurt they put on a shawl to go out for a walk. Did you think you were supposed to wear it in bed, Grandmother?"

"Well, Heidi," the old lady said, "I wear it in bed so I don't freeze. I'm really pleased with it as my blanket is a little thin."

"Grandmother," Heidi continued, "your head is going downhill, when it should be going uphill. That's not how a bed's supposed to be."

"I know, child, I can feel it," and Grandmother tried to plump up her thin pillow. "My pillow was never very thick, and I've slept on it for so many years it's become a bit flat."

"Oh, if only I had asked Clara in Frankfurt whether I could take my bed with me," said Heidi. "It had three big, fat pillows on top of each other. I couldn't sleep on them and had to slip down to where it was flat, but you're supposed to sleep like that there. Could you sleep like that Grandmother? Would you like to have three plump pillows?"

"Yes, of course. It would keep me warm and you can breathe more easily if your head is raised," said Grandmother, struggling to lift her head up. "But let's not talk about that now. I have so much to thank God for that other old and sick people do not have. There is the tasty bread roll that I get every day, and the lovely warm shawl here and the cakes you brought me. And best of all are your visits, Heidi. Would you like to read something to me today?"

Heidi ran out and soon came back with the old hymn book. She looked through one beautiful hymn after another, trying to choose one to read. She knew them all now and was glad to read them again, for it seemed a long time since she had heard the verses she had learned to love so well.

As she read, Grandmother lay back with folded hands and her face, which had looked so careworn, wore a happy smile as if she'd just been given something wonderful.

Suddenly Heidi paused.

"Grandmother are you feeling better?" she asked.

"Yes, Heidi. It makes me feel so much better. Would you read it to the end?"

Heidi read the rest of the hymn, which ended:

The darker my eyes grow
The brighter glows my soul
So I'll pass over gladly
As if I'm going home

Grandmother repeated this a few times, and her face had a look of happy expectation. Heidi felt very pleased. Suddenly, the sunny day of her own homecoming came flooding back to her, and she burst out joyfully, "Grandmother, I know just how it feels to be going home!"

Grandmother didn't answer, although she had understood. The expression that had pleased Heidi so much remained on her face.

"It's growing dark now Grandmother," Heidi said at last. "I must go home. But I'm so glad you're feeling better."

Grandmother took the little girl's hand and held it tightly. "Yes I am so happy again, even if I have to stay in bed a while longer, I still feel better. You see, nobody can really understand how it feels unless they've experienced it for themselves. I lie here so many days alone without being able to see so much as a single sunbeam. Then dark thoughts come over me and sometimes I think I can't go on. But then when you read these words to me, it's as if a light goes on in my heart, and I'm happy again."

Grandmother patted Heidi's hand and let it go.

Heidi sat behind him and away they went. They flew down the Alm as if they were a pair of birds sweeping through the air.

"Good night, Grandmother," said Heidi. Then she ran out in a hurry, pulling Peter outside with her, for night had already fallen. Peter pulled his toboggan straight and sat on the front. Heidi sat behind him and away they went. They flew down the Alm like a pair of birds sweeping through the air.

Later that night, when Heidi was lying in her lovely, high bed of hay by the stove, she thought of Grandmother in her uncomfortable bed, and then she thought of everything she'd said about the light going on in her heart. And she thought: if Grandmother could only have the hymns read to her more often, then she would feel so much better. But she knew that it could be a week or two before she was allowed to visit again. That seemed so terribly sad to Heidi, that she began to rack her brains for a way for Grandmother to hear the hymns every day. Then at once she had an idea. She was so excited about it she could hardly wait for morning to carry out her plan.

Suddenly she sat bolt upright in bed, for she'd forgotten to say her bedtime prayers. After earnestly saying prayers for herself, Grandfather and Grandmother, she fell back on the soft hay and slept deeply until morning.

Chapter Nineteen

The winter continues

In the days that followed, Peter came to school on time. He brought a packed lunch with him too. When the children who lived in Dörfli went home for their lunch, the children who came from further afield sat down at their desks, stretched their feet along the benches and spread out their lunches on their knees. When Peter had finished his first full school day, he went over to visit Heidi.

As he came in, Heidi shot over to him as if she'd been waiting for him, and said, "Peter, I know what."

"What?" he said.

"You have to learn to read."

"I already have."

"No Peter, not like that," said Heidi. "I mean learn to read so you can actually do it afterwards."

"I can't," Peter said.

"Nobody believes that any more, and neither do I," said Heidi determinedly. "Grandmamma in Frankfurt knew it wasn't true and she told me not to believe it."

Peter was astonished at the news.

"I can teach you," Heidi continued. "I know how. And you must learn so that you can read Grandmother one or two hymns every day."

"I won't," growled Peter.

This hard-headed resistance to something that was right and proper, not to mention dear to her heart, made Heidi see red. With flashing eyes, she came right up to Peter and said menacingly, "Then I will tell you what will happen if you don't ever want to learn anything. Your mother has already told you twice that you should go to Frankfurt to learn a thing or two, and I know where boys go to school there. As I was leaving, Clara showed me this huge, horrid house. But they don't only go there as little boys, they carry on until they're all grown up. I saw it myself. And then you mustn't think there's only one teacher like that at our school. There are whole rows of them, and they all go into this house, all dressed in black as if they are going to church, and have tall, black hats on their heads," Heidi showed the height of the hats from the floor with her hand, and a shiver ran down Peter's spine.

"Then you have to go in after all those teachers," Heidi continued emphatically, "and when it's your turn and you can't read and make mistakes with spelling all the time, then they will make fun of you, and it's much worse than Tinette making fun of you, and you should just hear how dreadful that is!"

"Alright I'll do it," said Peter, half pleadingly and half crossly.

Heidi calmed down immediately. "Good, then we'll begin," she said, pleased, and pulled Peter over to the table and fetched a book.

In the big package Clara had sent her, Heidi had found a little book with rhymes about the alphabet. The night before it had occurred to Heidi that she could use it to teach Peter how to read.

They both sat down with their heads bent over the book, and the lesson began.

Heidi told Peter to try reading out the first rhyme. He tried again and again, and in the end she said, "You can't do it, so I'll read it to you and then you'll know how it's supposed to sound."

So Heidi read out:

Learn your ABCs today,
Or the judge will call you up to pay.

"I'm not going," said Peter.

"Where?" said Heidi.

"To the judge to pay anything," said Peter.

"Then hurry up and learn the three letters, then you don't have to," Heidi advised.

Peter tried again, and repeated them persistently until Heidi said, "You must know these three now. Wait, I'll read you the other rhymes too and then you can see what's coming in our next lessons." And she began to read very clearly:

DEFG must come soon after
Or you'll suffer a disaster.

Don't forget HIJK
Or your luck will end today.

Whoever stumbles on L and M
Their friends will be ashamed of them

If you knew what waits for you
You'd rush to learn NOPQ.

If you stop at RST
Something's going to hurt, you'll see.

Heidi stopped there, for Peter was quiet as a mouse and she wanted to see what he was doing. All the threats and secret horrors coming had made such an impression on him that he couldn't move a muscle and sat there staring at Heidi.

Being a sympathetic soul, she felt sorry for him instantly. "Don't be afraid, Peter," she comforted him. "Just come every evening to me, and if you learn the same as you did today, you'll soon know your alphabet and nothing bad will happen. But you really have to come every day, not the way you go to school. Even when it's snowing."

Peter promised to do so, for the fright had made him biddable. Then he went home.

Peter obeyed Heidi completely. Every evening they studied the next letters and learned the rhyme by heart.

Often, Grandfather sat in the room and listened to the lessons, while he enjoyed his pipe. Sometimes the corners of his mouth twitched as he was listening, as if he was trying very hard not to laugh.

After lots of hard work, Peter was usually asked to stay for supper, which compensated him royally for the terror induced by the threats of the day's rhyme.

The winter days passed like this. Peter appeared regularly and made great advances with his alphabet.

But with each rhyme he acquired a new fear. They were at U now, and when Heidi read out the rhyme:

Whoever mixes up U and V
Will go to a place he doesn't want to be.

"As if I'd go there," grumbled Peter, but he learned the letters well, as if under the impression someone might at any moment haul him off to somewhere he didn't want to be.

On the following evening, Heidi read:

If you don't know W at all
Just look at the cane that's on the wall.

Peter glanced over and said scornfully, "Isn't one."

"But do you know what Grandfather has in the box?" asked Heidi. "A big fat stick, as wide as my arm, so if we take it out we could say, "Look at the stick against the wall."

Peter knew the stick very well. He bent over the book right away and learned the letter W.

The next day, it was:

If you want to forget X
You'll starve today and then the next.

Peter looked over at the cupboard where the bread and cheese were kept, and said, "I didn't say I wanted to forget X."

"Good, then if you aren't going to forget it, we can learn another today too."

Peter shook his head, but Heidi was already reading it out:

If at Y you stop to rest
Scorn will follow you at best.

At that, all the teachers in Frankfurt rose before him, with their tall black hats and mockery and scorn on their faces. He threw himself at Y and didn't stop looking at it until he could see it with his eyes closed.

The following day Peter came to see Heidi and was a little full of himself, as he knew there was only one letter left to learn, and when Heidi read out, "Whoever thinks by Z he's through, will be sent to Timbuktu," Peter scoffed, "Yes but nobody even knows where that is!"

"I'm sure Grandfather knows, Peter," said Heidi. "Wait here. I'll quickly go and ask him where it is. He's just at the pastor's house over the way." Heidi had already jumped up and was heading for the door.

"Wait!" Peter yelled fearfully, for in his imagination he saw the Alm Uncle and the pastor packing him off to Timbuktu, for he really didn't know what Z looked like. His yell stopped Heidi in her tracks.

"What's the matter?" she asked curiously.

"Nothing! Come back I want to learn my Z," Peter gasped.

"I want to know where Timbuktu is," said Heidi. "And Grandfather will be able to tell me."

But Peter made such a fuss that she gave up and came back. "You owe me something in return though," she said. Her face lit up. "I know, as well as learning your Z, we can start on sounding out syllables."

Peter groaned, but nodded his head. That evening, he learned so much that he made giant strides in his reading. And so they went on with the lessons, day after day.

The snow had softened again, and more snow fell on top of it every day, so that for three whole weeks Heidi wasn't allowed up to see Grandmother. It made her even more zealous in her lessons with Peter, so that he would be able to take her place in reading to Grandmother. One evening, Peter came home from Heidi's, walked into the hut and said, "I can do it."

"What can you do, Peterkin, dear?" asked his mother.

"Read," he answered.

"Is it possible? Did you hear that Grandmother?" Brigitte called out.

Grandmother had heard, and wondered how that could be.

"Heidi said I have to read you a hymn," Peter reported. His mother quickly fetched the book and Grandmother was very pleased, as she hadn't heard any hymns for a while. Peter sat down at the table and began to read. His mother sat by him listening, and after each verse she said, "Who'd have thought it?"

Grandmother listened to each verse very attentively too, but said nothing.

A few days later, Peter's class at school was doing a reading exercise. When it was Peter's turn, the teacher said, "We'll skip you as usual. Or would you like to try to spell out a line?"

Peter read three lines without stopping.

The teacher put his book down. He started at Peter in silent astonishment as if he'd never seen the like. Finally he said, "Peter, a miracle has happened. I've worked with you patiently for hours on end, but you weren't able to remember the letters of the alphabet, let alone read. Now, reluctantly, I've given up trying, and it seems that you have not only learned the alphabet, but also how to read, and very well too. Where did this miracle come from, Peter?"

"From Heidi," he answered.

With great astonishment, the teacher looked at Heidi, who was sitting innocently on her bench, not looking out of the ordinary at all. He continued, "I have seen a change in you, Peter. Whereas before, you stayed away from school sometimes for whole weeks at a time, recently you haven't missed a day. Where did this positive change come from?"

"From the Alm Uncle," was Peter's answer.

The teacher looked in great astonishment from Peter to Heidi and back to Peter again. "Very well then, once more please," he said cautiously. Peter tried out his reading skills once more on the three lines. It was true. He had actually learned to read.

As soon as the school day was over, the teacher went over to see

the priest to tell him what had happened, and what good effects both Heidi and the Alm Uncle were having on the community.

Every evening Peter read out a hymn at home. This far, he obeyed Heidi, but he never went any further. Grandmother never asked him to either.

Brigitte was full of amazement that Peter had reached this level of achievement. On some evenings, once the reading was over and the reader in bed, she found herself saying again to Grandmother, "I can't get over my happiness about little Peter learning to read like that. Now you never know what he might be able to make of himself."

Grandmother answered with, "It is so good for him that he's learned to read. Still, I'll be truly happy when spring comes and

Heidi can come to visit again. It is as if he's reading different hymns altogether somehow. Something in the verses is missing when Peter reads them, and I always have to wonder what it is, and then I never reach the peaceful state of mind I have when Heidi reads the words."

This was because Peter adjusted his reading a little so that it wasn't too much trouble for him. If he saw a word that was a bit too long or looked too difficult, he simply left it out. He thought Grandmother wouldn't notice two or three words missing from a verse, for there were plenty of other words in them. In the end, almost all the nouns were missing from the verses when Peter read them.

Chapter Twenty

Friends from afar

May had arrived. Streams trickled from the mountains down to the valleys and the mountain was bathed in warm, bright sunshine. It had turned green once more; the last of the snow had melted and the first little flowers, awoken by the sunshine, were peering out of the fresh grass. Up high, the spring breeze shook the old pine trees, which shed their old dark needles, allowing the young, brighter green ones to show. The eagle swept through the blue sky again, and all around the Alm hut warm sunshine had dried the last damp patches on the ground so one could sit wherever one pleased.

Heidi was on the Alm again. She leaped here and there and

couldn't decide which spot was more beautiful. First she listened to the wind blowing deeply and mysteriously down from the clifftops, until it reached the pines and shook them, and it sounded as though the wind was crying out in happiness, and Heidi did so too, and danced here and there in the wind like a leaf. Then she ran back to the sunny spot in front of the hut and sat on the ground and examined the short grass to find out how many flowers had opened their petals. So many little beetles and bugs were hopping and crawling and dancing around in the sun and enjoying themselves, just like Heidi. She took great deep breaths of the fresh spring air that wafted up from the freshly sprouting ground and thought the Alp had never been more beautiful. The thousands of tiny creatures must have felt as good as she did, for they seemed to hum and sing, "On the Alm! On the Alm! On the Alm!"

From the workshop behind the hut came a busy sawing and hammering, which made Heidi happy, for it was the homely old noise she knew well from the start of her life on the mountain. She jumped up and ran into the workshop to find out what Grandfather was making. He'd already put one new stool, all finished and ready outside the workshop door, and was busy making another two.

"Oh I know what you're doing," Heidi called out happily. "We'll need these when they come from Frankfurt. This one's for Grandmamma and the one you're making now is for Clara, and

then... then there must be another person coming," she faltered. "Grandfather, you don't think Miss Rottenmeyer is coming, do you?"

"I don't know," said Grandfather, "but it's best to have a stool ready so we can ask her to sit down if she does come."

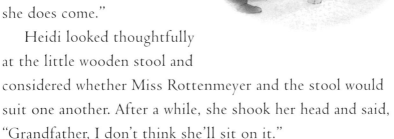

Heidi looked thoughtfully at the little wooden stool and considered whether Miss Rottenmeyer and the stool would suit one another. After a while, she shook her head and said, "Grandfather, I don't think she'll sit on it."

"Then we'll invite her to sit on the wonderful sofa with the grass-green cover," Grandfather countered calmly.

As Heidi looked around for the wonderful sofa with the grass-green cover, a whistling and calling and whirr of a stick being swept through the air came from above them. Heidi knew right away what it was. She shot outside and in a moment was surrounded by leaping goats. They must have been as pleased as Heidi to be back on the mountain again, for they jumped higher and bleated louder than ever. All around her they pushed and shoved, to try to get closer and show her how happy they were. But Peter scattered them left and right, for he had a message to give Heidi. When he'd pushed through to her, he held a letter out. "There," he said, leaving Heidi to work out where it had come from.

She was amazed. "You received a letter for me up there on the meadow?"

"No," he answered.

"Where did you get it from then, Peter?"

"From the bag of bread rolls."

It was true. The evening before the postman in Dörfli gave him the letter for Heidi. Peter had put it in the empty bag. In the morning he packed his bread and cheese in the back and went out. He saw Uncle and Heidi that morning when he'd picked up their goats, but it was only when he'd eaten his lunch of bread and cheese, and he was shaking the crumbs out of the bag that he'd remembered the letter.

Heidi read the address carefully, then bounded back into the hut and showed it to Grandfather in utter delight. "From Frankfurt! From Clara! Do you want to hear it right away, Grandfather?"

Of course he did, and so did Peter, who had followed Heidi inside. Peter took up a firm position, standing with his back against the door post, while Heidi read out the letter:

Dear Heidi,

We've already packed and in two or three days we're leaving, at the same time as Papa. He's not going with us, but has to go to Paris first. Each day the doctor comes and calls from the door, "Go! Go! Go to the Alps!" He can't wait for us to go. You must know how much he enjoyed being there himself. Almost every day all winter he's been coming to see me saying he just has tell me all about it again. Then he sits down and tells me all about the days he spent with you and Grandfather on the Alm, and the mountains and flowers and how peaceful it is up there, high over all the villages and streets, and about the fresh, wonderful air. He often says, "Up there a person simply has to get better!" He's so different again from how he was for a while. He looks so young and happy again.

Oh I'm so excited to see it all for myself, and to be with you on the Alm and get to know Peter and all the goats. But first I have to do a spa cure in Ragaz for six weeks, as the doctor recommended. After that we will stay in Dörfli, and each day when the weather is fine, I can be carried up the mountain in my chair and spend the day with you there. Grandmamma is coming too and staying with me. She's looking forward to seeing you up there as well. But guess what? Miss Rottenmeyer doesn't want to come! Grandmamma says almost once a day, "So what about the trip to Switzerland, my dear Rottenmeyer? Don't be shy about saying you want to join us." But Miss Rottenmeyer always thanks Grandmamma most politely and says she wouldn't like to presume. I know exactly what it is though. Sebastian returned from taking you there with such a frightful description of the Alps: how the fearsome cliffs loom overhead and how easy it would be to tumble down all the precipices, and that the mountain is so steep that you're terrified of falling with every step. He said only goats can climb around up there without fearing for their lives. Miss Rottenmeyer was so horrified by the description, it's put her off the trip completely. Tinette is scared too, and won't come either. So Grandmamma and I are coming alone. Sebastian only has to accompany us as far as Ragaz and then he can go back home.

I can hardly wait to visit you. Take care, dear Heidi. Grandmamma sends a thousand hellos.

Your loyal friend, Clara.

As soon as Peter had heard the end, he leaped outside and swung his stick left and right so angrily, that the goats all fled with fear and bounded off down the mountain. Peter stormed off behind them beating the air with his stick, as though fighting unseen enemies. These terrible enemies were in fact the guests from Frankfurt.

Heidi was so happy she said she had to visit Grandmother the very next day to tell her all about who was and wasn't coming from Frankfurt. Grandmother always took an interest in Heidi's life, and knew all about the characters from Frankfurt, so she'd certainly like to hear all about it.

The next afternoon, Heidi set off down the mountain. She was allowed to visit by herself now that the sun was shining and the days were longer. She ran down the mountain on the dry grass, with a May wind at her back pushing her along a little faster.

Grandmother wasn't in bed any more. She was sitting in her corner again, spinning. But the expression on her face suggested that she was having dark thoughts. Indeed this had been the case since the previous evening, when Peter had come home in a foul temper, and she had gathered from his angry silences and outbursts that an entire crowd of people from Frankfurt were coming up to the Alm hut. What would happen next he didn't know, but Grandmother came to her own conclusion, which was what had kept her up all night worrying.

Heidi bounded in, sat on a stool next to Grandmother and told her everything with great enthusiasm. But then suddenly she stopped in the middle of a sentence, and said, "What's the matter, Grandmother? Aren't you happy about it all?"

"Of course I am, Heidi," she answered, trying to look pleased. "I'm glad that you are so happy."

"But Grandmother I can see that you're worried... Do you think Miss Rottenmeyer is going to come?" Heidi asked, starting to worry herself.

"No, no. It's nothing," Grandmother reassured her. "Give me your hand, Heidi, so I can properly tell you're still here. It will all be for the best, even if it's hard to endure."

"I don't want anything for the best if you can hardly endure it, Grandmother," said Heidi.

And a new anxiety sprang up in Grandmother's mind. She had been worried the people were coming from Frankfurt to take Heidi back now she was healthy again. But now she felt that she had to keep her anxiety from Heidi. The little girl was so sympathetic that knowing how Grandmother felt might keep her from going with them, and that would never do. She tried to think of a solution but there was only one she could come up with: "I know, Heidi," she said. "It always makes me feel better and lifts my thoughts if you read me a hymn. Could you read the one that begins 'Good will come'?

Heidi knew the old hymn book so well now, that it didn't take her long to find the place, and her voice rang out as she read:

Good will come of everything
And healing won't be far.
Let the waves crash all around
and know how safe you are.

"Yes that's just what I needed to hear," said Grandmother, relieved. The worried expression disappeared from her face. Heidi looked at her thoughtfully, and then said, "Grandmother, healing means when a person gets better again, doesn't it?"

"Yes, that's how it will be," Grandmother nodded, "you can trust in God that he will make it so. Read it again, Heidi, so we can remember it."

Heidi read the verse a few more times. She liked the part about feeling safe.

Evening had come and as Heidi wandered back up the mountain, star after star came out and began to twinkle down on her. It was as if each one shone a new beam of happiness into her heart, and Heidi had to stop every few steps and look up at them. Scattered over the sky, they seemed to look down with ever-brighter joy, until Heidi called out to them, "Yes, I know. God makes everything turn out for the best, so you can just be happy and feel safe."

The little stars twinkled and sparkled down on Heidi all the way up to the Alm hut, where she found Grandfather standing looking up at them too. It had been a while since they had looked quite so beautiful.

Not only the nights, but the days too, were brighter and clearer than they had been in years. Often Grandfather looked on with amazement as the sun rose in another cloudless sky with a grandeur equal to the sunset the night before. He kept on saying, "This is an unusually sunny year. It'll give special power to the plants." To Peter, he said, "Watch out your goats don't get too boisterous on the good food, Chief!"

Peter swung his stick through the air and said boldly, "I'll keep them in check!"

So May flew by, and June came with even warmer sunshine and long, long, light days, which brought all the flowers out on the Alm. The air was filled with their sweet scent. June too was almost over when, one morning, Heidi came bouncing out of the hut having finished her chores. She wanted to go and see if the big bush of centaury had bloomed yet, as the flowers looked so delightfully pretty in the sunshine. But as Heidi ran around the side of the hut, she suddenly screamed with all her might, which was so unlike her, it brought Grandfather running out of the workshop in concern.

"Grandfather, look!" the little girl called, quite beside herself. "Come here and look!"

Grandfather turned his gaze in the direction of Heidi's outstretched arm.

Up the Alm came a strange procession, unlike any seen there before. First came two men carrying a sedan chair, in which was sitting a young girl wrapped in lots of blankets. Then came a horse, with a refined looking lady sitting on it. She looked around in a lively manner, talking energetically to the guide who was walking at her side. The empty wheelchair was carried between two porters, both of whom had luggage on their backs. The last porter was carrying so many blankets and rugs and furs heaped on top of one another that they towered far above his head.

"It's them!" screamed Heidi, jumping for joy. It really was them. They came closer and closer and then they were there. The porters put the sedan chair on the ground, and Heidi flew at Clara. The two children were utterly overjoyed to see one another. Then

Up the Alm came a strange procession, unlike any seen there before. First came two men carrying a sedan chair, in which was sitting a young girl...

Grandmamma was at the top, and got down from her horse. Heidi ran to her and said hello very lovingly. Then Grandmamma turned to the Alm Uncle who had come over to welcome her. There was no stiffness in their greeting, for they felt they already knew each other.

Right after she had said hello, Grandmamma exclaimed, "My dear Uncle, what a heavenly place you have here! Who would have thought it. Even kings would envy you this. And see how my Heidi looks! Like a rose in bloom!" She pulled Heidi closer and stroked her fresh cheek. "What magnificence all around. What do you think, little Clara?"

Clara looked around in utter delight. She had never dreamed of such beauty in all her life. "Oh it's lovely, Grandmamma," she said. "I never imagined it was this beautiful. I wish I could stay here forever!"

"I think it's better if we sit the little daughter in the wheelchair now, as the sedan chair is rather hard," said Grandfather, who had wheeled the chair over.

Grandfather didn't wait for anyone else to help, but picked Clara up in his strong arms and put her very carefully on the softer chair. Then he straightened the blanket over her knees and arranged her feet very gently on the footrest, as if he had done nothing else but care for the sick his whole life.

Grandmamma had watched with amazement. "My dear Uncle," she burst out now, "if I only knew where you'd learned your nursing skills, I could send all the serving staff there for training. How is it that you know such things?"

The Alm Uncle smiled a little. "It's more from experience than training," he said, but despite the smile his face looked sad. From a long-ago time, he remembered the suffering face of his captain, who had been so mutilated after a battle he had lost the use of his limbs. The Alm Uncle had found him on the battlefield, and carried him back. Afterwards, he was the only person the captain would allow near him, and the Alm Uncle had cared for him until the end of his days. He saw it now as his duty to care for Clara in the same way.

The sky stretched deep blue and cloudless over the hut and over the pines and the high cliffs. Everything Clara could see filled her with delight, and she drank it all in.

"Oh Heidi, if only I could walk with you, around the hut and under the pines," she cried out longingly. "If I could only go and look at everything with you. I feel as if I know everything and yet have never seen it before!"

Heidi heaved herself against the wheelchair and rolled it slowly across to the pines. She stopped under them. Clara had never seen anything like the tall, ancient trees with their long, drooping branches that almost touched the ground. Grandmamma followed the children over and stood there, overawed. She didn't know what was more lovely about the old pines: the rushing tips up in the blue sky or their straight, solid trunks that rose straight as pillars, with their great, spreading branches. For years and years, they must have looked down on the valley, where the people came and went and everything changed, while they remained the same.

In the meantime, Heidi had wheeled Clara over to the goat stall and flung open the door, so Clara could see inside. There wasn't that much to look at, as the goats were not at home.

"Oh Grandmamma," Clara called mournfully, "if only we could wait for Little Swan and Little Bear and the other goats and Peter! I can't see them all if I always have to go home so early, like you said. That's such a shame!"

"Dear child, let's enjoy all the lovely things we have and not think about the things we don't have," said Grandmamma, following the wheelchair as Heidi pushed it along.

"Oh the flowers!" Clara cried out. "Whole bushes of such tiny red flowers, and all the nodding blue heads. If only I could get out and pick some."

Heidi ran over right away and brought a big bunch back with her and laid them in her friend's lap. "This is nothing, Clara," she said, "If you come up to the meadow with us, then you'll see. There are so many in the same place – bushes of red centaury and lots more harebells than here, and thousands of bright yellow rockroses that looks like real gold shining on the ground. And then there are the ones with the big petals, that Grandfather said are called ox-eyes, and those brown ones, you know, with the round heads, that smell so good, and it's so pretty there! If you sit down you can't bear to get up again, it's so lovely."

Heidi's eyes sparkled with longing to see what she was describing and Clara lit up, reflecting Heidi's fiery longing in her own soft blue eyes.

"Oh, Grandmamma!" cried Clara. "Can I go? Do you think I would be able to get up that high?" she asked wistfully. "If only we could go, Heidi, and clamber around on the mountain together."

"I can push you there," Heidi assured her, and to show how easy it would be, she gave the wheelchair such a shove that it nearly flew down the mountain. Luckily, Grandfather was standing nearby and stopped it in its tracks.

While Heidi had been showing Clara around, Grandfather had been busy. Inside the hut, the pot on the fire was steaming and the huge toasting fork was over the coals. The table and stools were outside by the bench, and everything was ready for lunch. Before long, Heidi and Grandfather had brought all the food to the table, and everybody sat down to eat.

Grandmamma was utterly delighted by their

open-air dining room, from which she could see far over the valley and across all the mountains to the blue, blue sky. A mild breeze cooled the diners and whispered through the pines so pleasantly, it was almost like music.

"It's really heavenly here," Grandmamma said over and over again. "But what do I see here?" she asked in wonder. "Is that your second piece of toasted cheese, Clara?"

There was indeed a second piece of golden cheese on Clara's slice of bread.

"It tastes so good, Grandmamma. Better than the food in Ragaz," Clara said, taking a hearty bite.

"Go right ahead," the Alm Uncle said good-naturedly. "It's the fresh mountain air," he added. "It encourages the appetite where cooking fails to."

So they ate their meal very happily. Grandmamma and Grandfather got along very well and their conversation grew more and more lively. They agreed upon everything about people and things and the way of the world, so that it seemed as if they were old friends. A good while passed, and then Grandmamma noticed evening was approaching.

"We must be going soon, Clara," she said. "The sun is already on its way down. The porters will be coming back soon with the horse and sedan chair."

Clara's face, which had been so happy, looked suddenly sad.

"Just one more hour, Grandmamma," she begged. "We haven't

even seen the hut and Heidi's bed and everything. If only the day had ten more hours in it."

"That's probably not possible," said Grandmamma, although she wanted to see inside the hut too. So they stood up from the table, and the Alm Uncle steered the wheelchair to the door of the hut. But it was too wide to go through the opening. The Alm Uncle didn't hesitate. He lifted Clara out of the chair and carried her inside in his strong arms.

Grandmamma ran here and there inside the neat and tidy hut, looking at everything with great pleasure.

"This is your bed up here, Heidi, isn't it?" she asked, climbing up the ladder to the hayloft. "It smells so lovely. That must be a healthy place to sleep!" she said thoughtfully. She went over to the round window and gazed at the view. Grandfather came up the ladder with Clara, with Heidi hopping along behind.

Clara was completely beside herself with delight. "Heidi, you've got such a wonderful bedroom," she cried. "You can look right out into the sky from your bed, and you're surrounded by the lovely smell and can hear the pines outside. I've never seen such a lovely bedroom."

Grandfather looked over at Grandmamma.

"I've had a thought," he said, "if Grandmamma is in agreement. I think that if we kept the little daughter up here with us, then she might gain some strength. You've brought so many covers and blankets with you that we can certainly make up a soft bed. And

Grandmamma must not worry, for I assure you I can take good care of Clara."

Clara and Heidi cried out like two little birds that had been let out of a cage, and Grandmamma's face lit up.

"My dear Uncle, you are a fine man," she burst out. "Do you know what I was just thinking? That a stay up here would definitely strengthen the child. But I was thinking it was too much to ask of you. But there you go, speaking my thoughts but saying it would be no trouble at all. Thank you, Uncle, from the bottom of my heart." And Grandmamma shook the Alm Uncle by the hand, holding on with both of hers. He shook hers back, looking very happy.

The Alm Uncle went into action right away. He carried Clara back down to her wheelchair, followed by Heidi who couldn't jump high enough for joy. Then he piled all the furs and blankets over his arm and laughed.

"It's a good job Grandmamma came prepared for an expedition in midwinter. These have come in handy now!"

"My dear Uncle, one should always be prepared!" came Grandmamma's lively retort, "We can only be grateful we crossed your mountains without a storm, and now my precautionary measures have come in handy anyway. We are agreed upon that."

During this little exchange, the pair of them had climbed up into the hayloft and began to spread out the covers, one on top of the other. There were so many that in the end the bed looked like a little fortress.

"Let a single haystalk poke through now if it dares," said Grandmamma, pressing her hand all over the bed. But the soft pile was so high that none did. Satisfied, she climbed back down and went out to the children, who sat together with beaming faces, planning everything they would do while Clara was on the Alm.

"How long can Clara stay for, Grandmamma?" asked Heidi. That was the big question the children wanted answered.

"I should ask Grandfather," Grandmamma replied. "He'll know best."

"I think four weeks is about right," said Grandfather. "Then we should be able to tell whether the mountain air is doing its duty or not."

The children shouted with happiness. The chance to be together for so long surpassed all their expectations.

Just then, they spotted the porters down below with the chair and the horse. When they reached the top, the chair bearers were told to turn right around and go back down. Grandmamma went to get on her horse.

"This isn't goodbye because you can come up every now and then to visit us and see what we're up to," Clara called. "That's so much fun, isn't it Heidi?"

Heidi could only answer by jumping for joy.

Grandmamma got on her sturdy packhorse, and the Alm Uncle took the reins and lead the horse with a sure hand down the steep mountain. When Grandmamma protested and said he needn't come so far, he replied that he would take her all the way to Dörfli, as the path was steep and not without its dangers.

Grandmamma thought that now she was alone, she would go back to Ragaz rather than stay in Dörfli, and then she could repeat the journey up to the Alm from time to time.

Before the Alm Uncle had returned to the hut, Peter came running past with his goats. When the goats saw Heidi they ran to her, and the next moment she and Clara were surrounded. Heidi named and introduced each goat to Clara as it poked its head above the jostling crowd.

At last, Clara met all the goats just as she'd longed to: little Snowflake and funny Goldfinch, Little Swan and Little Bear, and all the others right up to big Bullfinch. Peter stood there the whole time, casting dark glances at the happy girl.

When the girls cheerfully called, "Good night, Peter!" he didn't answer, but whirled his stick grimly in the air as though he wanted to split the girls in two. Then he ran down the mountain, with his herd following behind.

Clara's glorious first day on the Alm had come to an end. As she lay on her big, soft bed in the hayloft, with Heidi next to her, she looked through the round, open window right into the shimmering stars, and said joyfully, "Heidi it's as if we're in a carriage way up high, driving right up into the sky."

"Yes, and do you know why the stars are so happy they are

winking at us?" asked Heidi.

"No I don't. What do you mean?" Clara asked back.

"Because up there in the sky they can see how well God has everything planned out for people. They don't have to be afraid, and can be quite sure that everything will turn out for the best. They are so happy about it, they're winking at us. But you know, Clara, we mustn't forget to say our prayers, and to ask God to remember us when he's planning everything out."

The children sat up again and said their prayers. Then Heidi lay down and immediately fell fast asleep. Clara lay awake a little longer, for she had never seen anything as wonderful as the starry view from her bed.

In fact, she hadn't ever really seen the stars before, for she'd never been out of her house at night, and the curtains were always closed before the stars came out. Whenever she closed her eyes now, they sprang back open, to see if the two biggest stars

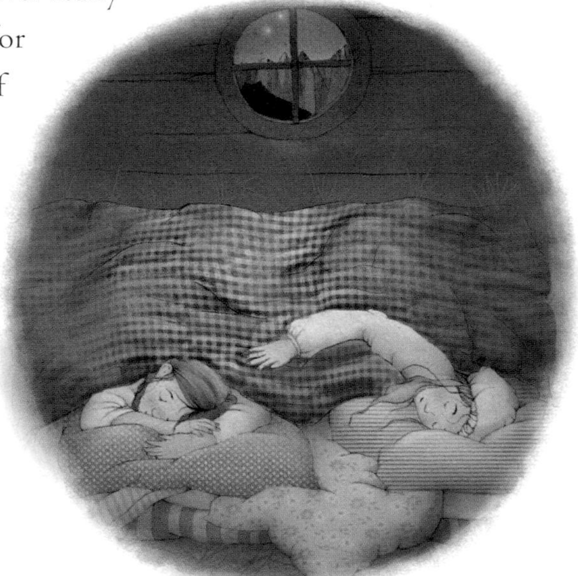

were still sparkling and winking in the sky. They always were, and Clara couldn't get enough of their glimmering and shining. Eventually, her eyes gradually fell shut, and Clara saw the two, big, shimmering stars in her dreams.

Chapter Twenty One

How life went on at Grandfather's

The sun was rising from behind the mountains and shedding its first rays over the hut and valley beyond. The Alm Uncle was standing by the door, as he did every morning, gazing quietly as the mists lifted and the night's shadows melted away. At last, the sun shone out, flooding everything with its golden light. Then the Uncle stepped back into the hut and went quietly up the ladder.

Clara had just opened her eyes and was looking in wonder as the sun came streaming in through the round window. At first, she couldn't think where she was. Then she saw Heidi sleeping beside her and heard Grandfather's friendly voice. "Did you sleep well?" he asked. "Are you feeling rested?"

"Oh yes," she replied. "I fell asleep straight away and didn't wake up once."

Grandfather seemed happy with this and gently began to help her get up. When Heidi woke, she was surprised to see Clara dressed and in Grandfather's arms, ready to be carried down. Heidi quickly dressed then rushed down the ladder and out of the door. There, she looked on in amazement. Grandfather had been busy the night before, taking down the boards of the shed so he could get the wheelchair under cover. Heidi came out just as he was wheeling Clara into the sunshine. Leaving her in front of the hut, he went to look after his goats, while Heidi ran up to her friend.

The fresh morning wind blew over them and Clara leaned back in her chair, breathing in the scent of the pine trees, feeling stronger than she ever had before. The sun was soft and warm. Clara had never imagined it would be like this on the mountain. "If only I could stay here forever," she said.

"Isn't it just as I told you," replied Heidi, delighted. "It's the most beautiful place in the world."

Just then, Grandfather came around the corner, carrying two mugs of foaming milk, one for each of them.

"This will do you good," he said to Clara. "It's from Little Swan. To your health!"

Clara had never tasted goat's milk before. She hesitated for a moment, sniffing the milk, but then seeing Heidi drink it up, she did the same, until there wasn't a drop left. It tasted delicious, she thought, sweet and spicy as if mixed with cinnamon and sugar.

"Tomorrow we'll drink two cups," said Grandfather, looking on with satisfaction.

Peter now arrived with his goats, who rushed up to Heidi in greeting. In their excitement, they bleated so loudly the Alm Uncle had to draw Peter to one side to be heard. "Let Little Swan go where she likes," he said. "She'll find the best food for herself, so if she wants to climb higher, follow her. It won't do the others any harm if they go too, nor you to do a little extra climbing. I want her to have the very best leaves and grasses so she'll give extra fine milk. Why are you looking over there, as if you wanted to bite somebody? No one will interfere with you. Off you go, and remember what I said!"

Peter went off, rolling his eyes as he went, to show he thought more than he'd said. For a little way, the goats pushed Heidi along, which was what Peter wanted. "You'll have to come with them," he called to her, "as I have to follow Little Swan."

"I can't," Heidi called back. "And I won't be able to come with you for a long time – as long as Clara is with me. But Grandfather's promised to take us both up the mountain one day."

As she spoke, Heidi made her way through the goats and ran back to Clara. Peter clenched his fists and shook them at Clara. Then he ran on up the mountain until he was out of sight, for fear the Alm Uncle might have seen him.

Clara and Heidi had made so many plans for the day, they

didn't know where to begin.

"Let's write to Grandmamma first," suggested Heidi. "We promised we'd write to her every day." Grandmamma had been a little worried about Clara's health, and whether staying on the mountain would suit her. She had asked for regular news so she could stay quietly at Ragaz, knowing she could quickly get to Clara if she were needed.

"Do we have to go inside to write?" asked Clara. She was so happy where she was she didn't want to move. But Heidi ran inside and brought out her school book and writing things and her little stool. She put her school book on Clara's knees, to make a desk for her, and pulled her stool up to the bench. Then they both began writing to Grandmamma. But Clara kept stopping to look around. The day was much too beautiful for letter writing, she decided. The breeze whispered lightly through the pine trees, insects hummed and danced around her. The pastures were quiet and still, while the high mountain peaks towered above her, lofty and silent.

The morning passed by in a flash. At midday, the Alm Uncle came out with two steaming mugs, saying he wanted Clara to be outside as long as it was light. So they ate, as yesterday, out in the open air. Then Heidi pushed Clara's chair under the pine trees so they could spend the afternoon in the shade, telling each other everything that had happened since Heidi had left Frankfurt. Although nothing unusual had occurred, Clara still had much to tell about all the people Heidi had come to know so well.

They sat and chatted under the trees. The more lively their talk, the louder the birds sang, as if eager to take part in the conversation. The hours flew by, and all at once the evening came, and with it Peter, driving on the goats with a heavy scowl.

"Goodnight Peter!" called Heidi, seeing he didn't mean to stop.

"Goodnight Peter," added Clara, as he rushed after his goats without a word.

As Clara watched Grandfather take Little Swan to her stall to be milked, she felt suddenly impatient for her next creamy mugful of milk.

"Isn't it curious," she said to Heidi. "As long as I can remember I've only eaten because I've had to, and everything seemed to taste of cod-liver oil. And now I'm longing for Grandfather to bring me my milk."

"I know what that feels like," said Heidi, remembering the days in Frankfurt when the food seemed to stick in her throat.

Clara, who had never spent the whole day outside in the fresh air before, couldn't understand it.

When Grandfather at last brought her milk, she drank it so quickly she emptied her mug before Heidi.

"May I have some more?" Clara asked.

Grandfather nodded approvingly, and brought them each out another mug, along with some sweet-tasting butter spread thickly over two slices of bread. He'd walked over that afternoon to a herdsman's house, where the richest, yellowest butter was made, and brought home a big ball of it. He stood and watched them, pleased to see how much they enjoyed it.

That night, Clara went to bed expecting to watch the stars, but she fell asleep as soon as Heidi. She slept until morning, more soundly than she had ever done in her life.

The next day and the next passed in the same happy way, but the third brought a great surprise. Two stout porters came up the mountain, each carrying a bed on his shoulders and all kinds of snow-white bedding. The men came with a letter from Grandmamma to say the beds were for Clara and Heidi, and that Heidi was to have a proper bed from now on. She could take one bed with her when she went to Dörfli for the winter, and leave the other at the hut, so Clara would know there was always a bed waiting for her. Then she thanked the children for their letters, and hoped they would continue to write them.

Meanwhile, Grandfather had cleared the hay from the loft and helped lift up the beds. He arranged them so the children could still see out the window, knowing how much they loved the morning sun and the stars at night.

Down at Ragaz, Grandmamma was appreciating her daily news from Clara and Heidi. Clara was enjoying herself more each day. She wrote of Grandfather's kindness and care, of how merry and amusing Heidi was – much more so than in Frankfurt. 'My first

She wrote of Grandfather's kindness and care... 'My first thought each morning,' she wrote, 'is how glad I am to be here still.'

thought each morning,' she wrote, 'is how glad I am to be here still, with all my friends on the Alm.'

Reassured to hear that Clara was doing so well, Grandmamma decided to put off her visit a little longer, as the steep ride up and down the mountain would be a tiring one.

Every day, Grandfather tried to think of something new to help Clara gain in strength. He climbed up the mountain every afternoon, high among the cliffs, and came home in the evening with a beautifully scented bunch of leaves. He hung them in the goat shed, and when Peter came down with the goats, they tried desperately to reach them, standing on their hind legs and bleating loudly. But Grandfather shut the door against them. He had gathered the leaves for Little Swan alone, to nourish her, so that she might give extra fine milk for Clara.

It was now nearly three weeks since Clara had come up the mountain, and for the past few mornings, when Grandfather carried her down to her chair, he said, "Will you try to stand, just for a moment?"

Clara tried to make the effort to please him, but as soon as her feet touched the ground she clung to him and cried out, "Oh! It hurts so!"

Each day, however, Grandfather let her rest her weight on her feet a little longer.

The summer rolled on, with cloudless skies and brilliant sun, day after day. The flowers opened wide their blossoms and at night, the mountain peaks glowed crimson red. Heidi never tired of describing to Clara the glory of the sunset from the higher slopes, where the blue flowers seemed to turn the grass to blue and the scent of the bushes made you never want to leave.

One evening, as they sat under the pine trees, Heidi was overcome with a longing to see the higher slopes again. She jumped up and ran to her grandfather in the shed.

"Grandfather!" she called. "Will you take us up with the goats tomorrow? Oh! It's so lovely up there now."

"Very well," he replied. "But Clara must try her best again this evening to stand."

Heidi ran back with her good news, and Clara promised to try her very best. Heidi was so pleased and excited she told Peter as soon as she saw him that evening.

"Peter, Peter, we are all coming out with you tomorrow and we're going to stay up on the mountain the whole day."

Peter only scowled in reply and lifted his stick to strike at Goldfinch, who had done nothing to deserve it. Goldfinch leaped out the way, and the stick only hit empty air.

That night, Clara and Heidi climbed into their beds, full of excitement about tomorrow. They agreed to stay awake all night talking of their plans, but as soon as their heads touched their pillows, their chatter ceased. Clara dreamed of a huge field, so thick with blue, bell-shaped flowers, it was as blue as the sky. And Heidi heard a great eagle calling to her from the heights above, "Come! Come! Come!"

Chapter Twenty Two

The unexpected happens

The next morning, the Alm Uncle went out before sunrise to see what kind of day it was going to be. The higher peaks glinted red-gold, a light breeze lifted the branches of the pine trees, swinging them gently back and forth. The sun was on its way.

Gradually, the peaks grew brighter. The shadows lifted from the valley, a rosy light filling the shady hollows. Then morning gold flooded everything. The sun had risen.

The Alm Uncle wheeled the chair out of the shed, then went to call the children, to tell them to come and see the sunrise.

As he went inside, Peter came up the slope, the goats keeping a little distance from him. They didn't trust him as they did before. Peter was now so bitter and angry he'd begun to take it out on his herd, hitting out wildly with his stick.

Every morning when he passed the hut, there was Clara in her chair, and Heidi seemed to have eyes only for her. And it was the same when he came down in the evening. Heidi hadn't come out with the goats once this summer, and today she was only coming to keep Clara company. Peter knew she would stick by her side the whole time and the thought made him furious.

Peter looked over at the chair, on its high wheels, and decided there was something proud and disdainful about it. He glared at it, as if it were an enemy that had harmed him, and was going to do even more harm today.

He glanced around. There was no sound, no one to see him. He sprang forward like a wild creature, caught hold of the wheelchair and gave it a violent and angry push down the mountain. The chair rolled swiftly forward. In another minute it had disappeared.

Peter sped up the mountain as if he had wings, not pausing until he was hidden in a large blackberry bush. He didn't want the Alm Uncle to see him, but he did want to see what would happen next. He looked down and saw the chair, his enemy, going faster and faster down the slope. Then it began to tumble. Over and over it went, until finally, in one great bound, it dashed to the ground. Pieces flew in every direction – wheels, armrests, torn fragments of the padded seat. Watching it, Peter felt a stab of delight. He leaped in the air, laughing aloud for joy. Then he ran

He sprang forward like a wild creature, caught hold of the wheelchair and gave it a violent and angry push down the mountain.

around, leaping over bushes, only to come back to the blackberry bush, looking down at the chair and laughing again. He was beside himself with satisfaction. Now Heidi's friend would have to go home, he thought, and when Heidi was alone again she'd come out with him, just like old times. He hadn't yet thought of the wickedness of what he had done, or the consequences that might follow.

Heidi now came running out of the hut and over to the shed. Grandfather came behind her with Clara in his arms. The shed stood wide open. Heidi looked in every corner and ran from one end to the other, then stood still, wondering what could have happened to the chair.

"Have you moved the chair, Heidi?" asked Grandfather, coming up behind her.

"I've been looking for it everywhere," Heidi replied, her eyes growing anxious.

At that moment a sharp gust of wind blew the shed door back against the wall.

"Oh!" cried Heidi. "Maybe the wind has blown the chair away! If it's been blown all the way to Dörfli, we won't get it back in time to go up the mountain!"

"If it's rolled as far as that we won't get it back, for it'll be in a hundred pieces by now," said Grandfather, going round the corner and looking down. "But it's a curious thing to have happened," he added. "The chair would have had to turn a corner to have started down the hill."

"We won't be able to go today," cried Clara, "or perhaps any other day. I'll have to go home, I suppose, if I have no chair. Oh, dear, oh dear!"

But Heidi turned to her grandfather with a look of perfect confidence. "Grandfather will be able to do something, won't you? So it won't be as Clara says and she won't have to go home."

"Well, let's go up to the pastures as we planned, and then we'll see what can be done," said Grandfather. Both Heidi and Clara gave a shout of delight.

Grandfather went indoors, fetched a pile of blankets and put them down in the sunniest spot, and laid Clara down upon them. Then he fetched their morning milk, and brought out Little Swan and Little Bear.

"I wonder why Peter's not here yet," he thought, for he hadn't heard his morning whistle.

When the girls had finished their breakfast, he picked up Clara and the bundle of blankets in his arms. "Let's start," he decided. "The goats can come with us."

Heidi happily followed her grandfather, her arms around the goats as she walked. They were so overjoyed to have her with them again, they nearly squeezed her between them.

When they reached the goat pasture, they were surprised to find Peter's flock was already there, climbing over the rocks, and Peter with them, lying on the ground.

"Lazybones!" called Grandfather. "Why didn't you stop for my goats?"

Peter jumped up like a shot. "No one was up," he said.

"Have you seen the chair anywhere?" Grandfather asked.

"What chair?" Peter called back, his voice strangely flat.

Grandfather didn't say anything in reply, but spread out the shawls on the sunny slope and settled Clara down. "Are you comfortable?" he asked.

"As comfortable as in my chair," she said. "Thank you! And this is the most beautiful spot. Oh! It is lovely," she cried, looking around in delight.

"I'll be off now," said Grandfather. "You'll be safe and happy together. I've put the lunchbag in that shady hollow, Heidi. Peter will bring you as much milk as you want, and Heidi, make sure that it is Little Swan's. I'll come and fetch you just before evening. I'd better go now and see what's happened to the chair."

The sky was dark blue and cloudless. The great snowfields sparkled as if they were set with stars and the old mountain peaks looked solemnly down on them. The eagle soared in the high air and the fresh mountain wind blew over them as they sat on the sunny slope.

Clara and Heidi were too happy to speak. Now and then one of the goats came to lie down beside them for a while. Snowflake came most often, to nestle against Heidi, only moving when it was budged out of the way by one of the others. Clara began to get to know them all by name, learning their ways and their funny little faces.

The hours slipped by, and Heidi began to wonder if she might climb a little further, to see if the flowers there were as beautiful as last year. Clara wouldn't be able to go until Grandfather got back, and by then the flowers would be closed. Heidi's longing grew so strong, she couldn't resist it any longer.

"Would you mind, Clara," she said hesitantly, "if I left you for a few minutes? I would so love to see how the flowers look. But wait!" she added. She ran and picked some green leaves, then took hold of Snowflake and led her up to Clara. "Now you won't be alone," said Heidi, throwing the leaves onto Clara's lap and giving the goat a little push to show her she was to lie down near Clara.

"I'm quite happy to be left with Snowflake. Do go and see the flowers," said Clara.

Heidi ran off, and Clara began to hold out the leaves to Snowflake, one by one, who slowly ate them from her hand. Clara found a strange new pleasure sitting all alone on the mountain, with only a little goat for company. She suddenly

wished she could look after herself, and to be able to help others, instead of always having to be the one who sat still and was waited on. New thoughts came crowding into her mind, along with a longing to always live in the sunshine. She happily threw her arms around the little goat's neck. "Oh Snowflake," she cried. "If only I could stay here with you forever."

Heidi, meanwhile, had reached her field of flowers, and gave a cry of joy to see a mass of shimmering gold where the rockroses spread their yellow blossoms and above them bunches of bluebells nodded in the breeze. Heidi stood and gazed and drew in the sweet-scented air.

Suddenly she turned and ran back to Clara, arriving breathlessly at her side. "Oh you must come," she said. "It's more beautiful than you can imagine, and it might not look so lovely this evening. I think I could carry you. Do you think I could?"

Clara shook her head. "You're smaller than I am. Oh, if only I could walk."

Heidi looked around in search of something, and a new idea came into her head. Peter was still sitting above them, where they'd first seen him, and he was now looking down at them. He'd been sitting there for hours, watching them, as if he couldn't believe his eyes. Hadn't he just destroyed that hateful chair, so that Clara would have to go home? And yet, here she was, sitting on the grass next to Heidi.

"Come down, Peter!" Heidi ordered, catching his eye.

"No!" Peter called back.

"But you must. I can't do this on my own and you must help me. Come quickly."

"I won't come," he replied.

Heidi ran a little way up the slope towards him, then stopped and looked at him, her eyes flashing with anger. "If you don't come at once, Peter, I'll do something that you won't like. I mean it."

Her words filled Peter with dread. He'd done something wicked, but so far he'd thought he was safe, and that only he knew about it. But Heidi spoke as if she knew everything, and would tell her grandfather, who he feared more than anyone. What would happen if he found out about the chair? Peter gasped and stood up. "I'm coming," he said, as he made his way down to her. "But you mustn't do what you said."

Peter looked so terrified that Heidi began to feel sorry for him. "No, of course not," she said reassuringly. "There's no need to be afraid."

When they reached Clara, she told him to lift Clara under one arm, while she took the other. They managed to lift her, but Heidi was too small for Clara to lean on.

"Put your arm around my neck, and your other arm through Peter's, then we'll be able to carry you."

But Peter had never done it before, and when Clara tried to put her arm through his, he kept his hanging down like a stick.

"That's not the way, Peter," said Heidi. "Make your arm into the shape of a ring, then Clara can put hers through it and lean her weight on you. Whatever you do, don't let your arm give way."

But they made little progress. Clara wobbled heavily between them, and Peter was taller than Heidi, so Clara was up on one side and down the other. She tried to use her feet a little, but each time she quickly drew them back.

"Try putting your foot down firmly just once," suggested Heidi. "Perhaps after that it won't hurt so much."

"Do you think so?" asked Clara, timidly. She tried one firm step on the ground, and then another. She cried out a little as she did it, then set down the other foot again, a little more softly.

"It didn't hurt so much that time," she said happily.

"Try again," urged Heidi.

Clara went on putting one foot after the other, until she exclaimed, "I can do it, Heidi! Look! Look! I can make proper steps!"

"Can you really walk by yourself? Can you really? If only Grandfather were here."

Clara carried on, still leaning heavily on Heidi and Peter, but with every step she felt safer.

"You can walk now, Clara. You can walk!" Heidi cried. "Now we can come up here every day and go where we like, and you'll be able to walk about just like me. You won't have to be pushed about in your chair and you'll get strong and well. It's the best thing that could have happened!"

Clara agreed. She could think of nothing better than to be strong and to be able to walk like other people, and no longer have to spend every day in her chair.

They didn't have to go far to reach the flowers, and as they came to the harebells, Clara said, "Could we sit down here? Just for a little while?"

So they sat down in the middle of the flowers on the warm mountain grass. Clara watched the flowers waving in the wind, with Heidi beside her. Heidi wanted to shout for joy that Clara was cured. But Clara sat in silence, for the beauty of the mountains had cast an enchantment over her, and there was no room in her heart for words.

Peter also lay among the flowers without speaking, for he was fast asleep. The breeze came blowing softly over the rocks and passed whisperingly through the bushes. Heidi got up now and then to run about, trying to find the best spot to enjoy the flowers' scent. So the hours slipped by.

It was long past noon when a small troop of goats came wandering through the flowers, with Goldfinch as their leader. They had come in search of Peter who had never stayed away from them for so long before. As soon as Goldfinch caught sight of him, he bleated loudly, alerting the others, and they all came trotting towards the children. Peter woke up, rubbing his eyes. He'd been dreaming that he saw the chair again, with its beautiful red padding, standing by Grandfather's door, without a scratch.

And as he woke he thought he was looking at its brassy nails, but it was only the bright yellow flowers in the field. He felt a shudder of dread again that he might be found out somehow. After that, he let Heidi order him about as she pleased, giving his help to Clara without a murmur.

When they reached their first spot, Heidi ran to get the lunch bag. She took out the food and divided it into three portions, pleased to see there was enough for all of them. Her threat to Peter this morning had been to deny him his share of the food, only in his guilt he had misunderstood her.

After sharing out the food, she sat down beside Clara, and all three ate well after their morning exertions. But there was too much food for Clara and Heidi, so Peter got to finish theirs. He ate every last crumb, but there was something missing. Every mouthful seemed to choke him, and he felt as if there were something gnawing inside him.

They ate so late, they didn't have long to wait before Grandfather came to fetch them. Heidi rushed to meet him, wanting to be the first to tell him the good news. She was so excited she could hardly get the words out, but Grandfather soon understood, and his face lit up. He rushed up to where Clara was sitting. "We have tried and we have won!" he said with a smile.

Then he lifted Clara up, putting his left arm behind her and giving her his right to lean on. She walked a little way, and with his strong arm around her, she trembled and hesitated less than before. Heidi skipped along beside her and Grandfather looked as though some great good fortune had come to him. Then he took Clara in his arms. "We mustn't overdo it," he said. "It's time we went home." And he went down the mountain path, anxious to get her to bed after such a tiring day.

When Peter got to Dörfli that evening, he found a large group of people crowded together, jostling to peer over each other's shoulders. Wondering what they were looking at, Peter elbowed his way through. There lay the remains of Clara's chair, scattered across the grass, the red padding and bright nails showing how fine it had once been.

"I was here when the men began carrying it up," said the baker, who was standing near Peter. "It must have been worth a fortune. I can't think how it came to break like this."

"The Alm Uncle said the wind might have done it," said a woman, busy admiring the red padding.

"Well I hope no one's to blame for it," said the baker again. "Or he'll be in a lot of trouble. When the gentleman in Frankfurt hears about it he'll want to find out what's happened. I'm glad I haven't been up the mountain for two years, as they'll suspect anyone who's been near that hut."

Everyone began to talk about it, but Peter had heard enough. He slunk away, then ran home as fast as he could, as if someone were after him. The baker's words had filled him with fear. He was sure a policeman would soon come from Frankfurt and ask about the chair, and everything would come out, and he'd be seized and put in prison.

By the time he reached home, he was so terrified he couldn't open his mouth to say anything. He wouldn't eat his potatoes, but crept off to bed as quickly as possible, then hid under the bedclothes, groaning.

"Peter must have given himself a stomachache by eating sorrel again," said his mother. "Just listen to the noises he's making."

"Give him extra bread tomorrow," said Grandmother. "He can have some of mine."

As Clara and Heidi lay in bed that night, looking out at the stars, Heidi said, "I've been thinking what a good thing it is that God doesn't give us what we ask for, even if we pray and pray for it, if he knows there's something better for us. Have you felt like that?"

"Why are you asking me that tonight?" asked Clara.

"Because when I was in Frankfurt, I prayed so hard to go home. And when I wasn't allowed to go, I thought God had forgotten me. But now I know that if I'd come away earlier, you would never have come here, and never have become well."

"But Heidi," Clara began, thinking hard. "If that's true... If God always plans something better for us than we know, we should never pray for anything."

"You mustn't think like that," said Heidi, eagerly. "We must go on praying for everything, as then God knows that we haven't forgotten that it all comes from Him. If we forget God, then He lets us go our own way and we get into trouble. Grandmamma told me so. If He doesn't give us what we ask for, we mustn't think He hasn't heard us and stop praying. We must keep praying and say, 'I am sure you are keeping something better for me, and I won't be unhappy, as I know you'll make everything right in the end'."

"How did you learn all that?" asked Clara.

"Grandmamma explained it to me first of all. Then when it all happened just as she said, I found it out for myself. I think Clara," she went on, sitting up in bed, "we ought to thank God tonight that you can walk now, and that He has made us so happy."

"I'm sure you're right. I was so happy, I almost forgot my prayers."

The next morning, Grandfather suggested they write to Grandmamma and ask her to pay them a visit, as they had something new to show her. But Heidi and Clara had another plan in mind – to prepare a great suprise. Clara was to keep trying until she could walk alone. Only then was Grandmamma to see her. Grandfather thought it would take Clara about a week, so their next letter to Ragaz contained a pressing invititation to visit them in a week's time, but they didn't say why.

The following days were some of Clara's happiest on the mountain. She woke each morning with a voice within her crying, "I am well now! I am well. I don't have to go about in a wheelchair.

I can walk by myself like other people."

Everyday she found the walking easier, and could go farther. And the more she walked, the more her appetite grew, so that Grandfather began to cut her bread and butter a little thicker and filled and re-filled her mug with foaming milk. He nodded was satisfaction to see it all disappear. And so another week went by, until the day came when Grandmamma was to come up the mountain again.

Chapter Twenty Three

Goodbye – until we meet again

The day before she was to start her journey, Grandmamma sent off a letter to the Alm, so her arrival wouldn't take them by surprise. The next morning, Peter brought the letter as he came up with goats. The Alm Uncle was already outside the hut with the children, Little Swan and Little Bear at his side. He looked first at the rosy faces of the children, then at the sleek, healthy goats, and smiled contentedly.

As Peter drew near his steps slowed. He timidly held out the letter to the Alm Uncle, but as soon as it had left his hand, he ran away, glancing over his shoulder as if afraid something might be after him.

"Grandfather," said Heidi. "Why does Peter behave like

Bullfinch does when he thinks someone might be after him with a stick?"

"Perhaps Peter thinks he deserves a beating," replied Grandfather.

Peter ran on until he was out of sight, then stood still and looked around him. Suddenly he jumped and looked behind him, as if terrified someone was about to seize him. At any moment, he expected to see a policeman from Frankfurt leaping out from behind a bush, and the suspense was weighing on him.

After Peter had gone, Heidi began tidying the hut so that everything would be spick and span for Grandmamma. Clara sat and watched her, and so the hours passed by unnoticed, until it was almost time for Grandmamma to arrive. Then the girls went outside and sat on the bench, eagerly awaiting her.

Grandfather joined them, showing off the bunch of blue gentians he'd gathered that morning on the mountain. He carried them into the hut. Every now and then, Heidi sprang up to see if there was any sign of Grandmamma.

At last she saw the procession winding up the mountain. First there was the guide, then Grandmamma on a white horse, and last of all the porter with a heavy bundle on his back, piled high with rugs and blankets. They came nearer and nearer, and when they reached the summit Grandmamma looked at the girls, sitting side by side. "Clara!" she cried out, hastening to dismount. "Why aren't you in your chair? What *are* you all thinking of?"

Then, as she came a little closer, she threw up her hands in astonishment. "Is it really you? Your cheeks are so round and so rosy. I hardly recognized you." She was hurrying forward to hug her, when Heidi slipped down from her seat. Clara leaned on her shoulder and together they began calmly walking together. Grandmamma looked on in amazement. Then laughing and crying at once, she ran to them. She embraced first Clara, and then Heidi, and then Clara again, unable to speak for happiness.

All at once she caught sight of the Alm Uncle, looking on and smiling. She took Clara's arm in hers and went up to the old man. Then letting go of Clara's arm she seized his hand.

"My dear Uncle! How can we ever thank you! This is all your doing. Your care and nursing..."

"And the sun, and the mountain air," he interrupted her.

"And don't forget the beautiful milk," added Clara. "Grandmamma you can't imagine how much goat's milk I drink, and how delicious it tastes."

"I can see that by your cheeks," replied Grandmamma. "You have grown strong and plump, and taller too. I never dared hope you'd look like that. I can't take my eyes off you, I can hardly believe it. But now... I must tell your father to come back from Paris at once. I won't say why. It will be the greatest happiness he has ever known. How can I send a telegram from here, Uncle? Have the men gone back yet?"

"They've gone," he replied, "But if you're in a hurry I can

fetch Peter, and he can take it for you." And he went aside and whistled so piercingly through his fingers that it echoed off the rocks. A few minutes later Peter came running down, for he knew the sound of the Alm Uncle's whistle. He looked white as a ghost, thinking now he was going to be punished. Instead, he was only given a piece of paper, and instructions to take it at once to the post office in Dörfli.

Peter went off with the paper in hand, relieved he hadn't yet been marched off by a policeman.

The others sat down for their lunch at the table outside the hut, and Grandmamma was told everything that had happened. "I can't believe it!" Grandmamma kept interrupting. "It's like a dream. Are we really all sitting here on the mountainside? Is that healthy-looking child really my poor, sick Clara?"

Clara and Heidi beamed with delight that their surprise had been such a success.

Meanwhile, Mr. Sesemann had been preparing a surprise of his own. He had finished his business in Paris and one sunny morning, without a word to anyone, he'd got on a train, filled with longing to see his daughter. He arrived at Ragaz only a few hours after his mother had left, and when he'd heard she'd started for the mountain, he'd hired a carriage to Mayenfeld. From there, he had begun the walk to Dörfli, and up the mountain.

He found it long and tiring. He walked up and up, but still no hut came into sight. The narrow footpaths seemed to run in every direction, and he began to worry if he'd taken the wrong one. He looked around to see if he could ask anyone the way, but there wasn't a soul to be seen. The only sound was the mountain wind and insects humming in the sunshine. Mr. Sesemann stood for a while to let the cool alpine breeze wash over him. Then ahead, he saw someone running down the path – it was Peter, with the telegram in his hand. He beckoned to the boy and Peter came forward with a sort of sideways movement, as if he could only move one leg properly and had to drag the other after him.

"Is this the way to the hut where the old man and Heidi live?" he asked.

In reply, Peter could only moan in fear. In his hurry to get away, he tripped and fell, and went tumbling down the mountain very much like the chair. The telegram flew from his hand and was carried away by the wind.

"How timid and shy these mountain people are!" thought Mr. Sesemann, thinking the boy must had been scared by the sight of a stranger.

He watched Peter tumbling down the valley for a few moments, then went on his way.

Peter tried to stop himself, but he tumbled on and on, more frightened by the thought a policeman had come to get him, than by his fall. At long last, he stopped, caught in a bush, on the last high slope above Dörfli.

"Well, well!" said a voice above him. "I wonder who'll be blown off the mountain next, and come rolling down like a sack of potatoes." It was the baker, who stood there laughing.

Peter sprang to his feet and began hurrying up the slope again. The baker sounded as if he'd known what had really happened to the chair. Peter wished he could go home and hide in his bed, but the Alm Uncle had told him to hurry back so the goats wouldn't be left alone for too long. He didn't dare disobey the Alm Uncle, so he went groaning and limping up the slope.

Meanwhile Mr. Sesemann continued his climb and at last, after a long and exhausting walk, the Alm Uncle's hut came into view, with the dark tops of the pine trees waving above its roof.

Mr. Sesemann chuckled at the thought of his daughter's surprise, but it was not to be. He had already been spotted by those outside the hut, who were busy planning a surprise of their own.

As Mr. Sesemann stepped in front of the hut, two figures came towards him, a tall fair girl and smaller, darker one.

Mr. Seseman stopped suddenly. He stared at the two children. Tears started in his eyes as memories stirred in his heart. As he looked at the tall girl he was reminded of Clara's mother, who had the same fair hair, the same pink cheeks. He hardly knew if he were awake or dreaming.

"Don't you know me, Papa?" Clara called. "Am I so changed since you last saw me?"

Then Mr. Sesemann ran to Clara and clasped her in his arms.

"You are changed!" he cried. "How has it happened? Is this real?" Mr. Sesemann stepped back to look at her again, as if afraid the image would vanish before his eyes. "Are you my Clara? Really my Clara?" he kept saying.

His mother came forward, eager to see her son's happy face. "What do you say now? You have given us a good suprise, but nothing compared to the one we had prepared for you, you must admit," and she kissed her son as she spoke. "But now," she added, "you must come and meet the Alm Uncle, and thank him for all he has done."

"Indeed," he said smiling. "And I must thank Heidi too," he said, shaking her by the hand. "Are you still well and happy in your mountain home?" he asked. "But I can see that you are. No alpine rose could look more blooming."

Heidi looked up at Mr. Sesemann's kind face and thought how good he had always been to her, and how glad she was he too had found happiness on the mountain.